ORDERED STEPS

ORDERED STEPS

Marriage did not enter the young missionary's mind until a stagecoach massacre made beautiful Marianne English his charge. How a spoiled aristocrat, a sanguine brother and a homeless house-maid—along with a praying mother—brought God's will in Perregrine Abelard's life will thrill you to tears.

LaJoyce Martin

Ordered Steps

by LaJoyce Martin

©1996, Word Aflame Press
Hazelwood, MO 63042-2299

Cover design by Paul Povolni
Cover art by Glenn Myers

All Scripture quotations in this book are from the King James Version of the Bible unless otherwise identified.

Printed in United States of America

Printed by

Library of Congress Cataloging-in-Publication Data

Martin, LaJoyce, 1937–
    Ordered steps / by LaJoyce Martin.
        p.   cm.   —   (The path of promise; 2)
    ISBN 1-56722-190-4
    1. I. Title.   II. Series: Martin, LaJoyce, 1937–   Path of promise;   2.
PS3563.A7248607   1996
813'.54—dc20   96-18966
                                                                                CIP

CONTENTS

Chapter One

The Travelers

The coach's curtain, fatigued and faded from its effort to keep the sun at bay, was looped back, allowing the evening light to fall across the four travelers. A more mismatched lot could not have been seined from the stream of life.

Despite the jostling of the stagecoach, Perregrine Abelard had slept away most of the trip; he was exceedingly tired. Now he roused, wondering how far they had journeyed.

"You won't sleep ery a wink t'night," predicted the pock-faced man beside him, who bore the marks of a bootlegger and an outlaw. He was a pigeon-shaped fellow with a large red lump for a nose. A few strands of hair lay flat on his head, combed across to hide his baldness.

"I think I could sleep a *week*, and it would seem but a *wink*." Perregrine gave a boyish grin. "Where are we?"

Mr. Flanders traced a grubby finger along the hand-sketched map tacked to the coach's interior. "Right about heresome, the best I can figger. Daresay the driver's tryin' to make it to the river 'fore dark."

"There's an inn there?" asked the overdressed lady on the seat opposite them. She was a statesman's wife traveling with her niece, Marianne, a porcelain-looking girl of nineteen. Mrs. English had the clipped voice of a woman who dictated her own terms to life.

Mr. Flanders snorted. "Of course, ma'am. With maids and butlers and a silver tea set. Right here in the middle of no-man's land. Just ring for service." His eyes were threaded with scorn. "Dream on, my dear lady."

She gave him a withering look. "I meant a modest lodge."

"This here's a new line, and there ain't no lodges," he blurted. "You an' the missus will have these here benches inside for to bunk the night on. Us men'll bed under the buggy with the driver. It's more'n fifty miles to ery a log cabin."

"Will it be . . . safe?"

"Will what be safe?"

"To park beside a stream and sleep in this wretched cart without protection," she flashed, angry at him for his callousness and angry at herself for making the trip without insisting on a list of accommodations.

"Nuthin's safe in this territory, ma'am. There's bears an' lions an' tigers—an' mayhap a hungry mosquito or two. Us men could take care of any of them dangers singlehanded. Except the mosquitos, of course. Can't do nuthin' 'bout their appetites."

"What about Indians?"

"This whole continent is their stompin' grounds, ma'am. They're bespread all over the countryside. The territory is theirn. Some er friendly, some ain't."

"But they all have a soul, madam," spoke up Perregrine. "And they need salvation."

"What they need," Mrs. English disdained acidly, "is to be taught to put away their savagery and to submit to their superiors."

"Their superiors?"

"The white man. Us."

"You are suggesting that we are better than they?"

"Of course. They have no education, no manners, no culture. As for me, I say we should domesticate this whole unrefined continent. My husband is formulating a motion to acquire *all* their lands. Don't you agree that this is a good idea, sir?" She looked to Mr. Flanders as a cohort.

"I'm afraid I'm on the dark side of politics, ma'am," Mr. Flanders protested. His hand strayed to the coat-concealed bulge with its forbidden contents. "I say the giverment should stay out of other people's business."

"Perhaps the natives have not had the chance for improvement that you in your privileged life have had," Perregrine pointed out.

"They are brutal! They are beastly! They are . . . They are . . ."

"And would you give up your home, your way of life and your food supply to be trampled underfoot in the dust of insult without a fight, madam?" Perregrine censured without raising his voice.

"If I had nothing more than a mud hut or a filthy animal skin, I wouldn't *bother* to defend it!"

"I'm sorry, but I cannot share your views. Their homes, however humble, mean as much to them as yours means to you. I came all the way across the ocean to preach—"

"You're a *parson*?" The feather on Mrs. English's Cossack hat doddered. She was a tall, crane-necked woman with her hair scraped back from a high-boned face.

"Well, yes. I have a burden for—"

"And so young?"

"I'm twenty-three."

"And unwed?" Mrs. English had forgotten about the Indians.

Perregrine blushed. "No. No, I mean yes. Yes, I mean no. No, no. I'm not married, that is."

Marianne's eyes were upon him, eyes so clear that they seemed to have their own weather. Her copper-gold hair was twisted into a rope and piled on her head. Loose strands tickled her nose, and she pursed her lips to puff them away. Perregrine was surprised by a fleeting dimple.

"Oooooh! How could we be so fortunate as to fall into the company of a parson?" Mrs. English smiled while Mr. Flanders wore his agony with dignity. "Marianne has been infatuated with parsons since she was a girl in pigtails and pinafores. Haven't you, Marianne?"

Now it was the girl's turn to blush. She said nothing.

"Actually, I feel a call to—" began Perregrine.

"Ah, a parson," swooned Mrs. English, cutting off any explanation he might have made. "I can just see you dressed in the cloth of a holy man, standing handsomely behind a carved podium with your sermon book in hand, your voice booming flawlessly with pulpit inflections."

"I've never—"

"Marianne would certainly complement such a ministry. Why, she can even sing a cappella."

"Sing a *what*, ma'am?" Mr. Flanders's already bulging eyes bulged the more.

"She has a heavenly voice for solo or accompaniment. Do you sing soprano or tenor in an ensemble, Reverend?"

"I—"

She waved her hand. "It doesn't matter. Marianne's voice will blend with anyone's. She would grace a rectory

12

quite admirably, too. And oh, she plays the pianola and the pump organ beautifully, Reverend. She is a most extraordinarily gifted young lady."

"I—"

"Have you preached at Swedes' Church? That's the oldest in Philadelphia, you know. They've just built Christ Church, and it's also a fine edifice. I say one church is as good as the next so long as it makes a good showing in the community. Marianne loves elegant sanctuaries."

Sensing Perregrine's discomfort, Mr. Flanders came to his rescue. "About them Indians, ma'am. We'll be trailin' midwise between two less-known tribes: the Ayutooks and the Kotopaxis. One is as harmless as a newborn babe, the other mean as the devil himself. Just hope them Kotopaxis don't smell us."

Mrs. English put her arm about Marianne as if to protect her from Mr. Flanders's startling information. "Don't talk so, please. I don't wish Marianne to be alarmed."

"I'm somewhat acquainted with the Kotopaxi tribe," Perregrine said, eager to keep the subject steered away from Marianne. "That is, I've been there."

"Oh, Reverend! Really? How that relieves my mind! Then you can negotiate with them if we run into problems?"

"I'm afraid not, madam. My experience wasn't a peace-pipe picnic. The chief shot at me, and I scarcely escaped death by his arrow."

"Pray, do tell us more, Reverend, ah, what is the name again?"

"Abelard. Perregrine Abelard."

"Quite an unusual name but lovely, to be sure. Are you perchance related to a Lewis Abelard who lives in Philadelphia?"

"He is my brother."

"How interesting! My, but he is a fine craftsman. He built my chiffonier."

"Yes, he has a talent for carving."

"He is the young gentleman I was telling you about, Marianne." Mrs. English's head pivoted from Perregrine to her niece and back again. "Marianne has not met your brother, Mr. Abelard. She has but recently arrived in America from the homeland. I am glad that it is you with whom she has made acquaintance. A parson is much more *professional* than a woodworker."

"I'm not—"

"But do continue your story about the encounter with the chief. How brave you must be! This is better than my nickel novels."

"There was no heroism on my part. I had gone into the woods to pray—"

"For your Sabbath day sermon, perhaps?"

"No, I was praying for the man who shot at me."

"How . . . how noble! How large spirited!"

"The chief was there before I knew it, riding his monstrous horse. Ere I could manage to scramble away, his arrow hit my hand. My wooden hand."

Mrs. English caught her breath in a gasp. She stared hard at the prosthesis.

"Oh, not *this* hand; this is a new one," continued Perregrine, following her gaze. "I gave the other to a child who needed it, and Lewis made me another. You see, I found asylum in the pueblo of an Indian woman named Lithia. She and her child were facing death for a lie she had told the chieftain. Her son was born with a handicap, and she told the chief that the gods would make the boy whole on his twelfth birthday. I was there the day before the deadline, and I gave the child my hand in the hopes that it would help. That was more than a year ago.

I've often wondered what happened to that troubled mother, though I felt a peace about it. I was able to share the gospel with her, and I know that whatever the outcome, she had a change of heart. It was the strangest thing: I was so certain that God had sent me to that particular tribe—and then the door closed after that single contact.

"So now I am on my way farther south to a tribe that has requested a Christian missionary."

The bright, false smile on Mrs. English's face died, and a frown was born to take its place. She hadn't taken her eyes from the wooden hand. "A missionary?" Her voice was thin and strained. "I don't think that Marianne would wish to marry a parson who would waste his time on heathens. And certainly not one with a wooden hand. I had in mind someone with a *brilliant future* for my niece."

"Pardon me, ma'am," interrupted Mr. Flanders. "I don't believe this here young man *asked* your Marianne for her hand in marriage. Leastwise, I didn't hear it if he did. I doubt if he'd want to be saddled with an aristocrat like her. I sure wouldn't!"

"Thank you, sir, for being my advocate," nodded Perregrine. He avoided Marianne's violet eyes, as innocent and disarming as a child's. "I have a work to do for my Master. I still cannot get the Kotopaxis off my mind, although I have convinced myself that the desire I had to reach them was born of my own human passion. I suppose one tribe is as deserving of the gospel as the next. Without a knowledge of the true God, the future for all of them is but a brief, empty prospect spilling over into eternity."

"Let's not talk of unpleasant things," insisted Mrs. English, holding up a gloved hand. "This is a pleasure trip for Marianne and me. Life is for the living; eternity is for the dead. I plan to live my full span and then some!"

"I was simply explaining that I have made a commitment to God, and I need no distractions," Perregrine said. "I'm afraid that even if I wished, I haven't the leisure to woo or wed."

Marianne seemed immune to the talk about her. The day's last ray of sunshine fell upon the girl, and she wore it in her hair, sparkling like a jewel. Perregrine thought that sunlight was made for her; it painted her a lustrous shade of clover honey.

Suddenly she laughed a tinkly laugh, like small shards of pottery falling on rocks.

Chapter Two

The Raid

They spent the night beside a nameless stream, a brisk rill that unraveled between brush and stones. Mrs. English grumbled at the inconvenience and discomfort. The driver did his utmost to make her comfortable before taking his place with Perregrine and Mr. Flanders beneath the stagecoach. "Women passengers are such a pain!" he was heard to mumble before sleep caught him. "Why can't they stay at home where they belong?"

Perregrine slept well, but at daybreak he awoke abruptly with a dread that stripped away the luxury of a slow, natural awakening. He asked leave of the driver to go into the woods to pray, hoping to relieve the heaviness that had suddenly and inexplicably seized upon his heart. Something dark and unknown plagued him.

Mr. Flanders spoke up and urged—too quickly—that the parson take his liberty, offering to help the driver with any preparations that might be required for the morning departure. The telltale flask bulged beneath his coat.

"Prayin' don't float my canoe, preacher," Mr. Flanders said. "I never wasted a minute with talkin' to someone I couldn't look in the eyeballs."

Perregrine winced at his disrespect.

"But if you have a prayer to spare," the man continued, "you might splash it over to the girlie in there." He jerked his thumb toward the coach. "The woman's been giving the young'un the 'what for' for hours. Kept me awake most of the night with her carping. I'll be gladsome when we rid ourselves of them two."

"I'll be glad to pray for her," Perregrine offered, "and I'll pray for you, too." He failed to see the derision on Mr. Flanders's flushed face.

With each step away from the campsite, Perregrine tried to analyze his feelings. From what source could such misgivings spring? He reckoned with his own soul, paring it bare in search of secret sins. Had the close proximity with Marianne brought unholy thoughts or wishes to his mind? He could find none. Was his mother, back in the old world, ill? He had no such premonition. What about Lewis, his brother in Philadelphia? Lewis was probably philandering, but that was nothing more than usual. Lewis would be Lewis, riding on his mother's prayers to keep him from the clutches of Satan until judgment day. What, then, could bring such a crushing burden?

Across the stream, Perregrine's agony pushed him to his knees on a bed of dry leaves. Not knowing what to pray for or about, he simply groaned in travail. Time was forgotten in his wrestling match with the unknown enemy.

A scream brought him to his feet, feet that were running before he had time for rational thought. The frantic sound had come from the direction of the coach. He urged his short legs to greater speed, wishing they were longer.

The sight that he met turned his blood cold, then hot. Mr. Flanders lay face down with a feathered shank protruding from his back. A lone Indian, scarcely out of boyhood, aimed yet another arrow at the driver.

Disregarding his own safety, Perregrine bounded from the woods, flapping his arms and bellowing. He unstrapped the wooden arm, his only weapon, and flung it toward the Indian. Seeing him, the frenzied young man whipped his horse about and fled as if he'd seen a ghost. But not before Perregrine caught one long look at the Indian's face. It was a face he could never forget.

The driver, seething with pent-up anger, shot at the retreating Indian. The blast of his black-powder rifle spooked the horses. They bolted, trampling the driver beneath their hooves as they smashed the carriage against a tree and overturned it.

Numb with shock, Perregrine retrieved the hand that had thwarted the murderer. Then he returned to Mr. Flanders. The silence of death rested on his face. The flask's contents spilled out with a noxious odor. Perregrine lifted one of the flaccid hands starting to turn cold. His skin tightened with horror. It was his introduction to death.

Then Perregrine made his way to the driver, his soul crying out against the senseless slaughter. A powerful hoof had crushed the driver's head. He, too, was dead.

The wrecked vehicle lay splintered and still. No sound or movement gave hope of life. Perregrine wept bitterly as with his one good hand he clawed at the wedged door that imprisoned two more victims. It took him an hour to peel away the wood and get to the interior of the coach.

Mrs. English's eyes, touched with death's chill, peered from the eternity she had wished to ignore but a few hours ago. Never again would they flash with indignation or glow with love. Earthly appointments had ended. Her stylish hat dangled at a rakish angle from the head with its broken neck.

Perregrine removed the rings from her fingers and the diamond brooch from her breast. There was no need to leave them for the predators. He dropped them into his pocket; he would return them to her husband. He also retrieved her ermine handbag.

Marianne was crumpled into a heap, looking as small and ethereal as a wraith. The discovery of each body had distressed him, but the sight of the girl brought a stab of anguish for which he was not prepared. "Marianne! Marianne!" he grieved. "You were so young . . . and so beautiful." He reached out to touch her and found her skin warm and supple. He jerked his hand back as if he had trespassed on forbidden property. Was she actually *alive*?

A new thought accosted him. If the girl was indeed alive and injured, it would fall his lot to care for her. The idea made him panic; his throat constricted, and he couldn't swallow. He knew nothing about girls or their needs. Life had not afforded him a sister, a girl cousin, or a female playmate. What if Marianne was fragile and weak by nature? How would she survive in this uncivilized setting? Perhaps she would die in his arms. He shook his head in an effort to ward off the terrible possibility. He could not bear the thought of it.

When a little moan escaped the girl's lips, Perregrine looked about frantically. He needed to get her out of the coach, but a beam lay across one of her feet. It might take dismantling the whole contraption to free her.

Perregrine set to work, his mind tumbling and turning. He focused his attention on the pain in his muscles so the sickness in his stomach would not make him retch.

He would like to take the time to bury the dead, but if there was any hope for Marianne, she must be his priority. Let the dead bury the dead. That's what the Bible said. Besides the danger of another Indian attack, other factors demanded immediate action. Perregrine knew he must get the unconscious girl to a colony somewhere, somewhere to a woman, to a mother, or to a doctor. And how far that might be or how long it might take badgered his thoughts.

The morning ebbed away as Perregrine worked, while over the interminable hours the girl groaned and murmured. Her eyes remained closed. When he noticed an immense lump on her head, his own hand fluttered as if to shoo away any death angel that lurked nearby.

The days ahead of him clamored for resolve. If he was able to pull this delicate flower through, if he could get her to civilization, what would he do with her? Would she return to her people, or would she wish to remain with him, her rescuer? He couldn't keep her forever just because he saved her life, could he? A brief spell of delicious insanity that set his heart at variance with all that was sensible left him shaken. Duty and desire clashed for the first time. A companion? He had always envisioned himself alone and following his call.

No! He could not keep her! With a divided mind, he couldn't be devoted to any woman. Even the Bible warned that a double-minded man was unstable in all his ways. What was he thinking? He *wasn't* thinking. Marianne would be a misfit in his world, a world that placed him among the most primitive of God's creation.

Marianne was still in a faint when Perregrine lifted her from the wreckage. Breathing deeply of the scent of her hair, he laid her gently on the ground and set about to construct a crude sled that would serve as transportation for the girl. In the boot of the coach, he found her portmanteau, wondering how he would manage to tow everything. It would be a gargantuan task.

With only a skeleton of a plan to guide him, he set out along the river, throwing an apology over his shoulder to the unburied corpses left behind. Time was of the essence.

He stumbled along slowly, halting often to lift Marianne's limp body from the dragging slide to negotiate obstacles. By afternoon, the bones of his legs ached so that he had to force them to respond; they seemed to expand and contract within his skin. How would he ever get anywhere at this snail's pace? She would surely die before they reached help. Would it have been better to stay with the spoilage and hope for some form of rescue? Should he go back? Which would bring the quicker conclusion? Fear and weariness walked with him.

The air was larded with smells of fall: dry grass, rotting logs, pungent earth. There was a tiny trembling of the wind that wasn't quite a breeze. Perregrine hoped it didn't indicate a weather change. A change would not be welcome; a change might leave him stranded in the shadow of an unknown mountain with his comatose charge.

In reflection, Perregrine remembered that Marianne had said nothing on the stagecoach journey. Her aunt did all the talking. He had never heard the girl's voice, only a peal of laughter that fell somewhere between a crackle and sweet music. What was this girl really like? And if she died, how would he ever know? He found himself wishing, praying, that she would awaken.

But by that evening, Marianne had not roused. Perregrine sought a shelter for her for the night. He chose a spreading evergreen with limbs that formed a natural tent around the leathery trunk. It was perfect.

Marianne's foot, the one pinioned by the bar, had begun to swell, and he removed her shoe but left her stocking intact. It was such a tiny foot! He held it in his hand to warm it. Did a little smile caper across her lips, or did he imagine it?

A chilling wind moved in with the darkness. An inestimable distance away, a wolf started to cry, a forlorn and lonely sound. The trees lost their friendliness. It would be a long night.

Whatever clothing Marianne had in her grip could be used for cover. The trunk itself would help to fend off some of the wind.

Exhaustion fogged Perregrine's brain and cramped his tendons. He supposed he hadn't covered five miles. If Marianne did not rally, it might well be weeks before he reached a peopled camp. There was less daylight every day, and the air held a sinister omen.

Winter slept just around the corner. . . .

Chapter Three

News

Lewis liked Philadelphia. It was rich with opportunity for a craftsman; it was his city, offering the success he hoped to gain in this new country to which he had come with his brother, Perregrine.

The busy metropolis never slept. The rhythm of excitement throbbed in its veins. Here the ladies were bedecked in satins and laces with their hair harassed into complicated coiffures. Old men carried canes with ornate silver heads, and young men stepped proudly in their frock coats. They danced. They reveled. They laughed. Grief was an unwelcome guest. Frivolity and excess were accepted as graces; the city's reputation boasted hospitality and luxury.

Known as the city of brotherly love, Philadelphia was wickedly extravagant. Here one heard accents of all the world in the markets where government ladies shopped for their dinner parties. Tables preened in priceless array, and the food was fit not only for a king, but also for Philadelphia lawyers.

Lewis was courteous to the men and even more courteous to the women. He could afford chivalry; any one of the city's elite might be his employer tomorrow. Already he was learning to pick and choose his customers, and his name gathered fame as a creator of finely sculptured furnishings. He had moved from Germantown to the lavish Elfreth's Court on the Delaware River, which gave him a decided boost up the social ladder. His mailbox was filled with invitations envied by men much more affluent than himself. Now and then, his name had appeared in the society column of the newspaper.

Marie Abelard, Lewis's mother, once said that Lewis could "charm the angels right out of heaven." He charmed as naturally as he breathed. His was a vigorous and flamboyant handsomeness in no way lessened by thick, black brows and shiny raven hair that made an exquisite swoop in the front. He bore scant resemblance to Perregrine, who inherited the shorter stature and light features of the many generations of Abelards.

Lewis had crossed the ocean to keep an eye on his younger brother as protector and guardian. At least, that's what he tried to convince his mother and himself. However, he soon found that Perregrine's choice of locations held nothing in common with his own interests. Why his brother should wish to persuade the natives of beliefs they didn't wish to embrace was beyond Lewis's sanguine mind. "Each man to his own, and leave him alone" was Lewis's philosophy. For his quick blood and young nerves, everything was a game. Life was for playing. For partying. For enjoyment.

Neither prairie nor forest called to Lewis. He couldn't imagine anyone wishing to leave the comforts of the city, move west, and settle in an unpopulated spot only to die unknown and obscure. He vowed to keep an ear to the ground for Perregrine but to get on with a life of his own while he listened.

Tonight was another big party. He had made many good business contacts at these soirees. All politicians considered such gatherings grand and useful affairs. When people get together, drugged by good spirits and the feeling of fellowship, they agreed to things which, under normal circumstances, they would consider mad. There was nothing like a nice party for doing business. Besides, he'd heard there was a new attraction at the last dinner, a niece of Mr. English, the statesman, and he hoped he might be introduced to her this evening. Reports had it that she was quite fetching of both face and pocketbook.

Margot Payne would be at the bash to dog his steps, of course. She pursued him with tireless tenacity. Heretofore, it would have been suicide for his career to shun her; her father held an important seat in the legislature just under Mr. English.

Now the thought that Mr. English's niece might liberate him from the clutches of Margot brought Lewis a sweet reverie. He had hoped that Margot would decide to go back to England, but she had not done so. Correctly, he suspected that he was the reason she hadn't.

Lewis took a last look in the mirror, straightening his cravat. He liked what he saw; conceit was an extravagance that he could not deny himself. Carefully, he smoothed his new shirt, examining with pleasure the starched tucks, the seams, the buttonholes.

He was leaving his quarters in disarray, but he had left word for Robin to clean his rooms while he was out this evening. Robin, known to the exclusive tenants of Elfreth's as "Round Robin" because she went from apartment to apartment, worked for several of them. She was an olive-skinned girl of uncertain age and origin.

Lewis guessed her to be on the sunny side of twenty. She was a hard-working maid who required but a cheap wage. She was not in his stratum of society, so he rarely exchanged words with her. She was a trustworthy scrub-woman, and that was what mattered. He could not imagine her in anything but a coarse, faded chemise.

Margot Payne was waiting for Lewis in the receiving hall and looped her arm through his in a possessive fashion. She had the notion that she owned Lewis exclusively. "Come along, dahling!" she gushed. "Togethah we'll have a delightful evening, you and I. I was half afraid you'd play truant, you fickle fellah!"

"I did consider it," he kept a solemn face, "knowing that you would be here."

"Aftah we are married, I shall nevah, nevah let you miss a single pahty, deah! What would a ball be without chahming Lewis Abelahd?"

"Whoa, there, Margot! You know I'll never wed!" he chortled. "I must be forever free to charm all the lovely ladies. I'm afraid I am not made of durable enough material to withstand matrimony."

"Ah, but mah Lewis! I want nothing less than a chahmer! I've found none more chahming than you."

"Is Mr. English's niece here? I had hoped to meet her—"

Green jealousy flared in Margot's eyes. "She is *not*. Her uncle said she went along with her aunt for a sight-seeing jaunt."

"Have you seen her? Have you met her?"

"I have not. Nor do I care to." She batted her eyelashes at him. "What should it mattah to you, dahling?"

"Ah, it makes no matter. Women are just women, to be viewed and admired from a distance."

With all Margot's beguilement, she could not hold Lewis's attention that evening. Lewis tired of social butterflies rather quickly, and his eyes inquired after each newcomer, anxious for a fresh face. However, when no new face appeared to blot up his solicitations, his disappointment made him restless.

By and by, he excused himself to talk with a group of gentlemen, pitching Margot into one of her pouts. On a sudden whim, Lewis had decided he would rather lose business than cater to her fawning. He was sick of her; he couldn't abide her long nose and sooty eyes another moment. He certainly wouldn't be saddled with her for a mere contract. Life was too short for such an arrangement.

Lewis moved among the politicians with ease and grace, sampling the topics of each. None of the talk was vastly important, but he listened with steady courtesy. He was polite and well-liked and might have passed for a prince himself.

"Modern women, striving to be free and equal, will hasten the destruction of us all!" a bewhiskered politician from one group railed. Lewis, disinterested in the discussion of women's suffrage, moved on.

Eventually, he tiptoed into a conversation that piqued his curiosity. He heard only snatches of it. Then his ear caught certain phrases, and with a sharp tightening of his nerves, he began to listen.

". . . four passengers, and all of them gone," said one of the conversationalists. "Indians."

"And one of them was Mr. English's wife, you say?"

"Yes. And her nineteen-year-old niece, recently come to America."

"Were the others identified?"

Lewis moved closer to hear.

"Records at the coach house list a Mr. Flanders, and there was a missionary—"

Lewis drew in his breath. He felt himself tremble; his

heart beat rapidly. Was it Perregrine? Perregrine had left on the stage a fortnight ago.

"Pardon me, sir," Lewis spoke up. "I didn't mean to eavesdrop, but I fear that my brother may have been on that stage. His name was Perregrine Abelard, and he was a missionary. He left on the last run west."

"That's the one that met with the misfortune."

"I had not heard. Were they all killed?"

"Three bodies were found: two men and a woman. Two are missing," the informant said.

"The two missing were . . . ?"

"A man and a woman. We have not been informed who was murdered and who is missing."

"I must know the fate of my brother. We have a widowed mother in the old country who will need to be notified."

"The two who fled are likely dead too, sir. They say the massacre took place about fifty miles from any known habitation. My condolences, to be sure."

A wave of guilt washed over Lewis, almost overwhelming him. He had promised his trusting mother that he would look after his brother here on the new continent. If a tragedy had befallen Perregrine, his mother would charge it to his account and go to her grave in grief. And in a way, Lewis was responsible.

His mind swept back to something he didn't want to remember: the day of the wood-cutting accident when the ax he wielded slipped from his grasp and severed Perregrine's hand and part of his forearm from his body. Lewis considered himself, five years older than his brother, at fault. He should have been more careful, should have seen that the child was out of harm's way.

Perregrine was a good person—kind, sensitive, and godly—everything Lewis secretly wished to be but knew he wasn't. If anyone should live, the good should live. . . .

Surrounded by the frippery of the crowd, Lewis felt immeasurably alone. Margot rushed to his side, all coyness, and recognized the face of a troubled man. It was a side of Lewis that she had never seen and didn't like.

"Well, forevermoah, Lewis! The look of bothah on that face. Did you lose—?"

"I lost my brother!" He jerked away from the hands that tried to hold him. "He was on the stage that was ambushed."

"Your brothah? You mean the missionary? Ambushed?"

"Yes. His stagecoach was attacked by Indians, and I don't know if he is dead or alive."

"It was to be expected, of course, Lewis deah. Anyone who would forfeit his life for savages, well—"

"Stop!" Lewis's eyes blazed with an angry fire. "His life was not a waste! It was much more valuable than mine! What do I do but whittle petty furnishings from dead wood while Perregrine touches hearts."

"Oh, don't speak so, Lewis. You have a brilliant careeah with a glowing futuah, but your brothah—"

"I carve senseless figures for money while my brother gives himself away unselfishly to lift lost humanity from a depraved state!"

"No, Lewis deah, now listen to me." She reached for him, but he backed away from her.

"Leave me alone! I will find him, dead or alive! I will go to the ends of the earth if need be. I promised my mother—"

"Lewis, you are beside yourself. Do be sensible, my deah. You can't give up your futuah for a penniless paupah of a brothah. We have a mahvelous futuah, you and I togethah. My fathah says you will soon be rich."

"I don't care about money!"

"Howevah, you do care about *me*, don't you, Lewis?"

31

Lewis was gone. He had vanished before her eyes, headed west in search of Perregrine, set adrift in an utterly strange world, a world without friends, folly, or fortune.

Chapter Four

Awake

Marianne awoke three days after the accident. She glanced about desperately for something familiar, a lost child's look on her lovely face.

"Ah, at last, those eyes are open," Perregrine said, a note of cheer in his voice.

She focused her vision on him. "Sir," she said, "where are we, and what has happened?" The shock of her soft, bell-like voice spread through his body like ripples on a lake. Her dependence made him want to flee from some new and unknown emotion that tried to emerge.

"The stagecoach was attacked by Indians. You and I are the only survivors."

"My Aunt Eleanor was . . . was killed?"

"Yes." The honesty might plunge her back into blackness, but he could not evade her searching gaze, nor could he lie. "Yes. I'm sorry."

Marianne was quiet for so long that Perregrine became concerned. He didn't know what to say to comfort her;

33

the unhappiness in her wide and questioning eyes hurt him deeply. If only he could bear her loss, take her suffering. She turned her head away, and he heard a sniffle.

"Are you crying . . . dear?"

"No. No, I am not crying." With the back of her hand, she wiped away tears that streamed down her cheeks. Her attempt at bravery tore at his heart.

"It is all right to cry. I cried . . . when I found you and you were hurt."

"You did? Oh, whatever shall I do, Mister— Mister—? I've quite forgotten your name."

"My name is Perregrine."

"Such a long name!" The fountain of tears stopped as suddenly as it had come. "I can never remember it."

"Call me Perry, if you would like."

"What shall I do, Perry? Where shall I go?"

"We will get you back to your family."

"I have no family. My mother and father were lost at sea. That left me an orphan. I came to America to my Uncle Charles and Aunt Eleanor. And now Aunt Eleanor is gone, and I am a *double* orphan."

"But you still have your uncle, Mr. English, do you not?"

Marianne shuddered. Her lips whitened, and he heard a high, choked note of misery in her voice. "Oh, please, sir. Don't take me back to Uncle Charles! He is never at home, and his housekeeper is a wretched witch who scolds me! And the butler is . . . is wicked. I cannot trust him to be a gentleman. Oh, promise me you won't take me there!" New tears started, tears that made Perregrine's nerves the more frazzled.

"First, we must worry about getting you well and getting out of this wilderness with our lives," he said gently. "Your foot is quite swollen. I hope that it isn't broken."

Marianne looked at her foot, pied and purple, with surprise. "You carried me here?"

"I brought you on the sled. And I brought along your travel box, too. I knew you would want to clean up and change clothes when you were stronger."

"Oh, my trunk! You wonderful man! I have never met anyone so *royal!*"

Perregrine dared not tie her words to the hitching post of his heart. He tried to turn the conversation in another direction. "Suffering teaches one empathy for other sufferers," he said.

"I suppose so." Her conversation jumped about like an unpredictable cricket during her intermittent mood changes. "But please tell me what happened to Aunt Eleanor and the others. Tell me the truth; I can bear it. I lived through the death of both parents."

"I know only the conclusion of the matter. When I returned from my morning devotion in the woods, Mr. Flanders had taken an arrow through his heart. I saw only the last of the Indians, a young buck, preparing another flint for the driver. My yelling frightened him away."

"How . . . how were the others killed?"

"The driver fired his rifle at the escaping Indian, causing a runaway of the team. He died under the horses' hooves. The carriage broke loose from the fleeing steeds and crashed into a tree. Your aunt had no breath when I got to her. And I thought that you were . . . gone, too."

"I'm afraid I don't remember any of it. The last thing I recall is Aunt Eleanor saying that she wished we had never come. She said she'd demand the driver to take us back to Philadelphia."

"It is best that you don't remember."

"Aunt Eleanor never should have made the trip. She

was angry with Uncle Charles over something trivial. It was a 'spite' journey, and I'm not sure of our intended destination. Aunt Eleanor was like a little girl running away from home when she was punished; she wanted to go to the farthest place on the land from her husband and spend as much of his money as she could. She told me we would 'see the world' and make Uncle Charles sorry he offended her. I'm sure she planned on more pleasant accommodations along the route, though. She was upset that we had to sleep in the carriage.

"Aunt Eleanor was a dreamer. When things didn't happen as she mentally pictured, she was irate with everybody. I'm afraid I am quite like her in that respect. Uncle Charles says I am spoiled."

"Your aunt did a foolish thing, miss. She never should have brought you to this wild country. It is no place for a refined lady. But what is done is done, and we must think only of survival for ourselves."

"What shall we eat?"

"I will catch some fish for us."

Marianne turned up her small nose. "I don't like fish. They *smell*."

"There are plenty of nuts and roots this time of the year."

"I might eat them if you will peel them for me. And where shall I sleep?"

"Wherever we can find a place for you. In a cave or—"

A visible tremor passed over Marianne. "I will be terribly frightened, Perry. Will we come to an inn presently? I will be so grateful when we reach the city."

"Until you are able to walk, I'm afraid that our progress will be very slow."

"I can walk." She tried to stand but abruptly cried out in pain and fainted.

He bathed her pinched face with water from the brook, seized by a panic that they would not make it. When Marianne opened her eyes, she fretted. "Oh, Perry, you shall have to drag me on the sled the rest of the way! I cannot bear the pain. It is horrible! Please, I need a doctor. How much farther must we go?"

He sighed. "We must keep going until we find a settlement. *Any* settlement." He had not imagined that this child-woman, bright and beautiful as a flame, would put such a weight on his heart.

"You won't leave me, will you?" Terror parked behind the plea in her eyes.

"Well, no. I—that is—not until I find someone to care for you."

"Oh, you can *never* leave me, sir! I'm all alone in this world. I must have someone to care for me forever. Perhaps you will be obliged to marry me. If you were kind to me, I'm sure I could care for you."

"But I have my mission, my ministry . . ."

"Am I not as important as the . . . the natives?"

"Of course you are." A battle raged within Perregrine. "But . . . but I must obey my Lord."

"Couldn't you obey Him in the city? Couldn't you preach to the statesmen and the lawyers and the *Christians?*"

"My calling is to the lost. Would you be content with me as I go to the uncivilized people who live under primitive conditions?"

Marianne's face registered surprise. "After such creatures killed my aunt, the only mother figure I had? Would you ask that of me, Perry? *Would you?*"

"You must learn to forgive, Marianne."

Something in her accusing look made Perregrine feel like a cad for mentioning his burden. She had burdens enough without his. "Then could you live alone while I am away for several days at a time?" he asked. It might work.

An appeal replaced the surprise. "Since my father and mother were . . . lost, I can't bear to be alone. It's too . . . too dreadful."

She brightened for a small moment and gave him a melting smile that betrayed the dimple. He tried to follow her ups and downs, the valleys and mountain tops of her whims. "Since God placed me in your care," she said, "He must mean that I am to be your responsibility, don't you think?"

"I'll make it a matter of prayer. God will show me what to do."

Perregrine's mind seethed with turmoil. Marianne, with her silk-toned hair and creamy white skin, was a cultured creature. The rigors of missionary work were outside the periphery of her constitution. The Indians would not accept her, nor would she accept them. To care for her would require a change of lifestyle on his part; it would be unfair to expect her to make such a drastic reformation.

Could he adjust to the confines of high society? His type of ministry left something lacking for the upper crust, the educated. A city church would not vote for him. He would be obliged to look for a laborer's job, and who would hire a one-handed man with no marketable skills?

Yet Marianne's argument was valid. God had certainly placed her in his life, so God must expect him to do his best for her. He had not asked for the chore (or was it a privilege?), and it would not be proper to keep her with him indefinitely without a commitment. The quagmire in which he found himself oozed with confusion. What did God expect him to do?

He said little the rest of the day, feeling sliced in two

by his circumstances. A part of him was happy, a part saddened. He didn't want to forfeit his ministry for Marianne. Or was it that he didn't want to give up Marianne for his calling to the natives?

They covered a frighteningly short distance but found a cave for protection from a rainstorm that swept through the forest. As the day closed, the wind made a hoarse sound in the throat of the cavern. It shouldn't have bothered Perregrine, but it did.

When Perregrine fixed Marianne's bed of soft moss, he was bone tired. His mind was frayed, his emotions raw. Yet through the weariness, he was aware of a singular energy. It surged through him.

Somewhere along the trail today, he had made up his mind. He had no choice. When he reached civilization, he would find a parson to marry them. Then Marianne would belong to him. Forever. He would have someone to love him, someone beautiful. They would be happy.

He made his own bed between her and the cave's mouth. Nothing could reach her—man, animal, or element—without first passing over him.

Despite his fatigue, it was a long time before he was able to still his racing heart and sleep. Thoughts of Marianne swirled in his head. A lifetime devoted to trying to please her would not be long enough. He would try to give her what she wanted, what she needed.

At last, when he did fall asleep, he dreamed about the chief of the Kotopaxi tribe. The chieftain reached his hands toward Perregrine and implored. *Come . . . Come . . .*

Chapter Five

Marie's Decision

Two years had passed since Marie Abelard had seen her sons. Two lonely, anxiety-packed, mother-yearning years. Now she questioned the meaning of her life separated from all that was important to her by miles of ocean.

Why make gingerbread cakes with their sugar-webbed icing when there were no boys' hands to reach for them? Why milk the cow, churn the butter, and light the lamps for only Marie Abelard? Ringing the dinner bell was useless; no one came. Her closest neighbor lived acres away, and the hamlet held no charm for her. Her faithful husband had gone to his reward more than a decade ago. Since her sons were making their lives in the new country, why keep the empty homeplace?

Marie had entertained a feeble hope that her boys would not find America to their liking and would return promptly. Now she had to admit to herself that no such thing would happen. Lewis wrote glowing accounts of the country abounding with opportunities. If she wanted to see her children again, she must go to them. Her thoughts by day and dreams by night were filled with a mounting desire to set foot in the wonderful land that had swallowed her offspring.

After much prayerful deliberation, she put the house on the market. The money from the sale would adequately finance her trip and would see her modestly situated in America. She could endure the transplant; she wasn't old enough to mold yet. She wouldn't tell the boys her plans, though, lest they object. She would simply show up in America and surprise them.

There were a few things she would want to take along with her. She would need the big family Bible that recorded the marriages, births, and burials of the Abelards from years past because there would be more such recordings in the new country. She could not part with the vase Lewis had carved for her. It was his first project and had provided her with a revelation of his talent and his future. In addition, she would take along some special seeds.

Impatience nibbled at her good nature before the transaction was completed. Once she had made the decision to liquidate and cross the ocean, all other prospects dimmed. A ticket to America to see the faces of her sons was worth more than house, land, or sentiment. Not once did she doubt the wisdom of her actions even in the foul, crowded steerage of the ship, noisy with the babble of many languages. Acclaimed a "fine passenger ship," it turned out to be a pitiful cargo boat. One of the rear holds had been converted into makeshift berths, and the space was shared with several cows that had been brought along for meat. There were no chairs or benches on the deck. The food ladled out by the cooks was the most disgusting Marie had ever tasted, and it was served in unwashed, open trays.

But what did it matter? She would soon be with her loved ones!

She informed, questioned, and bored everyone on the sailing vessel with stories of her family and her marvelous destination. She stopped the cabin boy with his buckets of dirty water. She detained the boatswain. Before long, passengers and crew members hid when they saw her coming. Not a day passed without her how-much-longer query.

On the tenth day, the vessel ran into a violent storm, and the sailors went aloft to take in the sails. The wild lurching of the ship left most of the voyagers seasick, gray with terror. Some knelt on the floor to pray; others swooned on their cots. Many were so sick they voiced their wishes for the deliverance of death.

But Marie didn't get seasick along with the bulk of the wayfarers. She attended those too ill to care for themselves, but not without a nonstop discourse on the whys and wherefores of her journey. Whether or not they listened, she was compelled to talk.

Eventually, the storm blew itself out and fine weather returned, releasing Marie's captive audience to mobility again. The journey consumed fifty days.

Lewis had written that he worked in Philadelphia. Marie didn't know how she would like a big city, she told anyone who would lend an ear, but if she didn't like it, she had an option. She could join her younger son, Perregrine, in his mission work out in the "wild and woolly." Her boys were opposites, they were, and she figured to see the best of both worlds. And no, they didn't know she was coming. They had no *suspicion* that she was on her way. And yes, they would certainly be flabbergasted. She wasn't given to such daring expeditions. In fact, she had never traveled beyond her own village.

Hours before the ship dropped anchor, Marie was

sitting with her luggage piled about her feet in anticipation. She was the first one to catch a glimpse of the coastline, banked with warehouses and trees, and the first one down the gangplank when they anchored in the harbor. The trunk she heaved along at her side was almost as big as she was. "Git outta that woman's way, or she'll knock you to smithereens," a salty sailor hurrahed, jumping out of her way in mock alarm.

With her sea legs on solid ground once more, Marie looked about. "What a busy place," she murmured, surveying the shipbuilding and textile mills abustle with workers. "I wonder where everybody is going in such a hurry?" Then she looked about as though she expected someone to be there to greet her. How would she ever find her son, Lewis, in such a mob, and how could she ever become a part of this strange, forbidding land? In the midst of the bustle of the ships at anchor, the carrying of bales and barrels, fear bayed at her heels.

Alone, with no one to welcome or cheer her, she was seated on her trunk looking lost when a passerby asked if he could be of assistance.

"Yes," she said, drawing herself up to her full height. "At least, I hope so. I am here to see my son, and I haven't a notion which direction to go from here."

"What is your son's name, and on which street does he live?" asked the man.

"That information would be helpful, wouldn't it?" She gave an embarrassed little laugh. "His name is Lewis Abelard. He carves all sorts of things. And he lives at Elfreth's Court, wherever that might be."

The man touched the brim of his hat. "Everyone knows where Elfreth's Court is, madam. With all that Victorian gingerbread on its front and the cozy, mullioned windows looking out over the gardens, it couldn't be missed. That's where the fancy folks live. May I fetch your trunk there?"

"Please." Marie straightened her black cabbage of a hat, outdated and maligned with grime. "I'll be in your debt."

"Not at all." The gentleman collected her baggage, and she followed him, trotting to keep up.

However, when they reached the quarters, she found that Lewis was not at home. "He left last week," a neighbor informed her. "He went to see about his brother who met with an accident."

"An accident? Oh, I pray it isn't anything serious!" She sat down on the stoop of Lewis's apartment lest her unsteady legs betray her. "Now, what shall I do? Where shall I stay until he returns?" She expressed her thoughts aloud. "I suppose that he will bring Perregrine here. Oh, I do hope that he isn't *badly* injured. Poor, poor Perregrine. He has had more than his share of misfortunes in life. The devil is trying to deflect him from his mission."

The gentleman who escorted her still held the trunk, waiting for instructions. "We must hope for the best, madam. Is there somewhere I can deposit this luggage?"

"Just put it down beside me, sir. I'll have to wait here until Lewis returns."

The man set the baggage beside the door and hesitated expectantly. Some propriety lay just outside the perimeter of Marie's grasp. He cleared his throat, and she gave him a puzzled look. What did he want?

"Oh!" She blushed, fumbling in her purse. "Yes, of course. Your fee." She placed a coin in his hand, and he disappeared like a vapor.

Marie waited on the step for an hour. She grew hungry but had no idea where she might find an eatery. Fear that she would become disoriented and not find her way back held her by Lewis's front door. Besides, she had no desire to lug the trunk about with her, and she couldn't leave it behind and chance its getting stolen. It held all her life's belongings.

Another hour passed, and Marie grew fidgety and apprehensive. She had not reckoned on Lewis's being away when she arrived. "What shall I do, Lord?" she asked, looking skyward.

A richly clad girl minced down the walkway with her head high, her bracelets jangling. When she saw Marie in her outmoded hat, she stopped in her tracks. "Did you not read the sign?" Her question matched her arrogance.

"What sign?" Marie asked, innocently enough.

"The one posted on the side of the building. It says no tramps or vagrants. You had bettah move on. Important people live at Elfreth's."

Marie smiled her sweetest. "Yes, I know. My son lives here, and he is quite important. He carves things."

"You are speaking of . . . Lewis Abelahd?"

"None other." Marie's chin raised just a bit.

A crimson tinge added color to the young woman's already painted face. "Oh, Mrs. Abelahd, please do accept my apologies for being rude! You will undahstand, won't you, that many, ah, bothahsome people presume on the tenants of Elfreth's? All of us try to preserve their privacy—"

"I understand. And I thank you."

"I am Margot Payne, your son's fiancée." She gave a curtsy. "I am so pleased to meet my futuah mothah-inlaw. He has told me about you," she lied. "In fact, he mentioned recently that you would be coming."

"He did?"

"Yes, and oh, he was so very pleased to have his mothah visit!"

"I—I didn't tell him that I was coming," said a per-plexed Marie. "I wonder how he found out?"

Cornered in her prevarication, Margot stuttered her way out. "Uh, now that I recall, it may not have been *Lewis* who told me his mothah was arriving from—from Egypt, I believe?"

"Oh, no, no! I'm not from Egypt!"

"I do get things terribly mixed. We go to so many socials, Lewis and I, and meet so many lovely immi-grants to this delightful city. I can't remembah who is coming from heah and theah." She breezed on, satisfied that everything was in her control again. "And now that you have appeahed for a visit, Mrs. Abelahd, it will make life even more meaningful. Oh, but Lewis will be thrilled that you have come to be a guest at our futuah wedding."

"Wedding?"

"Lewis didn't tell you?"

Marie ran her hand over her hair, the hue of autumn sedge with the sun on it. "N-no. He didn't tell me. I came to *live* with Lewis."

"Oh, I'm afraid that would nevah work."

"But I didn't know, you see, that he planned to take a wife, and I've already sold my home."

"There's inexpensive housing across the rivah. Lewis and I will see you situated, to be sure. Lewis is quite too busy to care for you personally."

"When—?"

"We will be married when he returns from his broth-ah's. He left in a rush before we could finalize the plans."

"Can you tell me where he went so that I may go to him?"

"My deah lady, he went on some unimportant errand. If I knew where he was, I would join him myself. I came by today to see if perchance he had returned."

"I don't know what I shall do or where I shall stay until he gets back."

Margot Payne surveyed the older woman critically. The mercury of her temperament had dropped from polite to coldly polite, then to cold. "I should say it was an inopportune decision for you to appeah without informing your son. If I were you, I would make resahvations on the first boat back to youh homeland—and stay theah. At your age, theah will be evah too many adjustments in our fast-paced city."

Chapter Six

Robin

The noon sun hung high, warming a flock of clouds. Robin, her dark face an unreadable mask, came to Elfreth's Court to do her weekly cleaning. She found Marie Abelard asleep on the step, her head on the trunk, her cheeks stained with fresh tears.

Robin had a key to Lewis's rooms; he'd asked that she keep them dusted in his absence. She would have to bypass the sleeping woman to get to the door.

Robin knew the desolation of being hungry, of being frightened, of being alone. A chord of empathy echoed in her heart for this poor woman, whomever she was. "Mem . . ." she touched Marie's hand with a gentle caress.

Marie jerked herself upright, alarm clear in her eyes. "I-I . . . Where am I?"

"Thou art being in Elfreth's Court, mem," Robin said. "Art thou lost? Can I be showing thee to somewhere?"

"I-I came on the boat," replied Marie with a deliberate

effort to control her fear. "I came to see my son, but I find that he is gone."

"I am having nothing to offer thee, mem," Robin patted Marie's arm, "but thou can be going home to mine. Mine wage is stingy—and mine rooming. But if thou do not scare of wharf rats, welcome thee will being with me tonight."

"Why, you precious child! How unselfish! The last dame who came by told me I should hie myself back over the ocean. That I cannot do. I must see my sons. What is your name, dear?"

"Robin."

"That's the whole of it?"

"That's all I am ever knowing, mem. I am not knowing mine birth. I am once in a Quaker family, but the mem is dying already. I am scrubbing from that day on. Robin is all I am needing for a nobody like mine."

"My name is Marie, and I can pay you a shilling for a place to sleep until I locate my sons. Both of them are here in America somewhere."

"No money I am taking from thee, mem. Thy bedding will be a pallet and hard. I am sharing thee mine covering. Gladsomely, it is not cold yet. We will being fine. If thou wilt be sitting here while I am doing mine job, please." Robin pulled a key from her pocket and started for the door.

"You work for my son?"

"No. I am working for the man who is making carvings for the rich. He is a nice man." Hers was a face Marie could almost trust, a face she felt she already knew.

"Is his name Lewis Abelard?"

"Yes, mem. Thou art knowing him?"

"He is my son."

Now it was the girl who recoiled. "Thou, Mr. Abelard's mema, and I am offering thee a stingy! Now I am seeing thy son's face in thine. Oh, for pardon, mem! My face is being ashamed."

"You have nothing to be ashamed of. You are a dear, and I love you. I will go in to Lewis's rooms with you and help you clean."

"Oh, no, mem! Thou mustn't be lifting thy finger. Mr. Abelard is paying me good for the working. Here, leave me to be hefting thy crate in for thee."

Before Marie had time to object, the industrious girl had lifted the trunk up the steps and into the apartment. Marie followed, thanking God for answering her prayer. Inside Lewis's home, she could wait for him in serenity.

"Do you know where my son is and when he plans to return, Robin?" Marie asked.

"I helped him ready for the trip," Robin said. "His brother—he is not knowing if he is bad hurting. Maybe alive, maybe not." Seeing the anguish on Marie's face, Robin quickly added, "It will be fine. If dead his brother is being, by now Lewis is coming back. Long gone is good news, mem. No thou be worrying thy heart. I am keeping clean the house for thee till he is returning. Some I can be cooking. Thou art hungry?"

"My dear child, I am starved, but I will not have you waiting on me like a slave! Let us see what we can find in the cupboard, and we will share a meal together."

Robin drew in her breath. "Oh no, mem! Mr. Abelard might be angering if the girl of working is eating his food."

Marie threw back her head and laughed, a hearty, old-country laugh. "My dear child! Lewis is the most easy-going boy in the world . . . and the most generous. He would be unhappy if you *didn't* have lunch with his lonely mother. You see, Lewis had no idea I was coming. I came as a surprise, and he will be sad that he wasn't here to greet me himself. But when he finds that you were here *and* so kind, well . . ."

"I am no worthy like thee. When he is learning that I am inviting thee to mine shabby, he will be upsetting."

"You must not think such thoughts, dear. All souls belong to our Heavenly Father. He made us all, and we are of equal value in His sight: the rich, the poor, the large, and the small. I had much rather be in your company than the haughty girl who came by earlier." Marie frowned at the recall. "She says that she and my Lewis are to be wed. I cannot abide the dreadful thought."

"Thy son will be taking a wife for himself?"

"Now that I am here, I hope to discourage it."

"He is not saying anything nearing to it. He is not talking to change his rooms. He is saying I am working on and on only for him."

"That's good news."

Marie and Robin spent a pleasant afternoon together. Marie threw the windows wide to the cool air, washing the rooms of their musty smell. She found ground corn, oil, and cheese in the larder. She made corn fritters, regretting aloud that there was no molasses.

"I am never eating so much good," declared Robin, relishing the repast. "Thou art having a head for cooking." She tried to serve Marie, but Marie insisted on treating her as a comrade rather than a maid.

"So kind a mem, thou art," commented Robin. "I have no kind mem since the Quaker mem who is once loving me."

"And I have no daughter," Marie returned, "so we can keep each other company."

Robin dusted Lewis's rooms then prepared to go. She came to bid Marie good-bye.

Marie caught her hand and held it. "You cannot leave me alone tonight. I am in a new environment, and everything is different. Please stay with me so that I shall feel safe."

Robin shook her head. "It is too nice for me to be sleeping."

"Oh, fiddlesticks!" scoffed Marie good-naturedly. "It's too nice for me, too, but who cares? These are only *things!*" She flung her arms in a wide arch. "What is inside the heart is the thing that counts. Paul said he had learned to be abased and he had learned to abound. We can do the same, you and I."

Robin looked at her blankly. "Paul?"

"In the Bible."

"I am not knowing Paul. But I am knowing Mr. Abelard. He will be in a dark mood if I am staying with thee?"

"Lewis will be more upset if you leave me. He would not want me to stay by myself on my first night in America. There, you have that bedroom, and I'll have Lewis's room." Marie pointed. "Sleep is stalking me. And tomorrow, you shall take me to the market for food and supplies. My home belonged to Lewis for twenty-five years. Now Lewis's home shall be mine—and I shall pray that the shrew who came earlier today shall not disturb the peace around here." She stopped to catch her breath. "At least, I don't have to worry about Perregrine wedding the wrong woman. He will *never* marry."

Robin managed her rare smile. "Good night, mem." Had she ever been so indulged? She removed her outer layer of clothing and slipped under the covers. A feather mattress embraced her emaciated body, bringing glorious comfort.

As she fell asleep, the fingers of her memory reached for a face dimmed by years of separation: her own mother's face. The encounter with Marie Abelard had awakened a long-lost craving to know who she was.

What would it be like to be loved . . . by anyone on earth?

Chapter Seven

Firewood

The temperature dropped as a steady drizzle soaked the ground outside the cave where Marianne and Perregrine were sequestered. A bleak fog shrouded the trees, rendering their shapes opaque, transforming them into dense, shapeless phantoms. Little streams of crystalline water made musical sounds as they sought places to seep into the cold soil. A wedge of geese eased south, their calls amplified in the echoing enclosure. The wilderness was preparing for its winter life.

Perregrine always felt a dull pain in the amputated arm at this season, and now he added yet another ache, an ache that rode deep in his heart. The stab of frost was not far away. There was a draft in the cave as if the earth were breathing through some crevice. How would he keep Marianne warm?

"I'm cold, Perry," Marianne murmured. "I shall take an ague if I am not warmed. I am prone to colds and fevers. Everything is damp: my hosiery, my petticoat, and my covers. Can you not build a small fire to keep me warm?" The walls and ceiling of the small rock chambers gave her voice a hollow resonance.

"All the wood is wet," Perregrine replied. "It will not burn."

"Can you not find a stick of dry timber *anywhere?*" Agitation tinted her voice. It is the pain that makes her irritable, Perregrine told himself.

"I have searched diligently, my dear. You must try not to fret. Fretting avails nothing."

"But just a *tiny* fire would help. You don't want me to become ill, do you?"

"That is the last thing I would want, Marianne. You have problems enough as it is." He beat back his own frustration with mental fists. She depended on him with such childlike confidence, and he was letting her down. He would give anything to see that she was well taken care of. . . .

The solution, so obvious that Perregrine chuckled aloud, came like a flash of brilliant light.

"Why are you laughing, Perry? Being cold is not funny."

"I just thought of something. Something to warm you."

He would use his wooden arm for firewood! It was made of hardwood and would create an enduring heat with a bed of lasting coals. "We shall be cozy."

He unfastened the arm and set it afire. When the warmth pervaded their haven, Marianne immediately curled up and fell into a contented sleep. With her golden halo of hair framed about her face, she reminded Perregrine of an angelic being. He told himself that he was a most fortunate fellow to be betrothed to this fairy-tale princess. Theirs would be a storybook marriage.

However, he could not push the dream of the Kotopaxi chief from his mind. It haunted him. Far into the night, he wrestled with it, trying to expurgate it from his mind as the layers of time peeled back and he relived much of his brief life.

His feelings had always run deep. Lewis had laughed and played with careless abandon, but even as a small boy, Perregrine had sensed the presence of God and had taken seriously his responsibility to be sensitive to God's wishes. He pored over the family Bible when he was scarcely out of bibs. There was so much in God's Word that called to his soul. He wondered why those about him did not hear the call. Divine matters didn't seem important to Lewis. Lewis heard only the call of birds and a whittling knife and his merry friends.

If Perregrine's mother and Lewis did not attend church, Perregrine went to the vine-clad sanctuary alone. He showed up every Sabbath. Not Lewis! He used every imaginable excuse to stay home from church to frolic or whittle. Sometimes he would pretend an illness, and his mother would stay home with him.

It wasn't that Lewis was a bad child; the spiritual tuning key had never touched the strings of his heart.

When still on the tender side of twenty, Perregrine knew that he must go to the new country and its natives. It would demand a complete submission of self. He had not heard the divine voice thunder in his ears, but it had whispered to his heart. He could not have been more certain of the direction had words been spoken directly from heaven.

It was no surprise to his mother when he shared his burden with her. What was a surprise to them both, though, was Lewis's decision to go along with his younger brother to see that he didn't fall into a "scalping."

Lewis did not understand Perregrine's unworldly nature and had poked harmless fun at him over the years, but beneath Lewis's good-humored banter, he loved and respected his little brother and would defend him against the world. Woe be to anyone else who ridiculed Perregrine!

Looking over his shoulder from today, Perregrine supposed he had viewed the missionary work in America through the rose-colored glasses of youthful optimism. He envisioned whole tribes giving up their gods for the one true God. They would want to know salvation's plan and would eagerly respond to the gospel. He would lead them in droves to the waters of baptism.

Under what illusion he had been! Most of the Indian tribes were unresponsive, and some were downright hostile. He had met with evil spirits that he had not known existed. The powers of darkness were not willing to relinquish their subjects.

Once he had found a totem pole with gruesome faces hidden in the woods. It seemed that demons peered at him from the faces, challenging his right to be in the new land. With righteous indignation, he threw the idol into the river. But there were many more like it, and destroying one icon did nothing to stem the worship of idols.

Then there was the day he went deep into the woods to pray. Before he realized it, he was surrounded by Indian warriors. The chief, a fearsome hulk of a man, shot at him, striking his wooden hand with a heavy arrow. Snaking his way through the underbrush, Perregrine escaped and found refuge in the pueblo of a young widow named Lithia.

Lithia had one child, a boy born without a hand. Since the chief had a rule that declared any defective person or animal must die, Lithia hid her son for six years. When word of the boy's disability got out, she told the chieftain a terrible lie to save her child. The gods, she said, came to her in a vision and promised that her son would be given a magic hand on his twelfth birthday. That day was but a few hours away when Perregrine hid in her tent.

Perregrine had offered mother and son hope through a prayer-answering God. Then he gave his hand, the wooden hand that had saved his life, to Lithia's son.

Oh, that he might know what happened thereafter! His heart gave a lurch. He would never be able to return to the Kotopaxi tribe now. He had another mission in life, a different mission in a very different direction.

That "mission" lay sleeping at his feet. He smiled, a smile that was part thankfulness and part regret. He had come to the crossroads and crossed. . . .

Outside, the valley was swathed in translucent wisps of mist.

So was his future.

Chapter Eight

Essence

When Essence felt the gnawing emptiness, she walked aimlessly in the woods. Here she could lose herself in the scent of the air, the aroma of the pines. She could watch cocks as they rose from the ground ahead of her, their stubby wings beating a drum roll when they flushed. She liked to watch the glow of the setting sun tint the treetops and then the blue of twilight gradually replace the red of sunset. There had been times she had stayed in the forest all night to watch the stars shine, each sparkling with an ember of living fire. In the stillness, the moonlight, and the thousand shadows and reflections, she found a solace.

Today she felt especially closed in by the skins of her large teepee, so she braided her hair into a single rope and took the moccasin-worn trail that led to the river. Yesterday had been a day of mist and somber grayness. But the morning brought a truce between land and sky. As Essence walked, her fingertips came together, seeking out the shape of prayer.

Life had not been kind to the pretty Indian woman. Once married to the chieftain of her Ayutook tribe, Essence was now a widow. Her husband had been shot by the white man's fireball, but no bitterness lived to rankle in her soul. The white man had shot out of fear.

Not long after her husband's death, she had lost both of her children; she had been alone now for many years.

At forty-one, Essence could have remarried. No young girl in her tribe welcomed a comparison. At her side, youth appeared raw and flavorless. She'd had her chances, but none of the braves who pursued her brought a response within her heart.

She could be called a beautiful woman. Her eyes, set in webs of finely wrinkled skin, gave the odd effect of other eyes behind those one saw. When only a child, her father had told her: *Always carry the sun with you, inside of you, and you will never walk in darkness.* This Essence tried to do. A delicious aura of womanhood lay not so much upon her skin as inside it; the air around her took on a sheen that was there but wasn't visible. She was endowed with the rare gift of goodness. In a crisis, her tribesmen came to rely on her natural strength.

She had gone to keep house for her brother, chief of the Kotopaxis, for a while, thinking to ease her restlessness. He liked the johnnycake she cooked for him and was kind to her, but she disagreed with his policies. He warred with the white man. The Ayutooks lived in peace with the colonists. They were friends. They traded furs for books, tools, and new kinds of seeds. They even held feasts together.

From childhood, Essence had felt a great kinship with the settlers. Her father, looking into the future, had sent her to live in a log cabin with a white family for several months so that she might learn their language. "We will need to communicate with them," he reasoned.

"You, Essence, are young and quick-witted. You can learn more swiftly than an adult. You will be our interpreter." With fluent English, she became the negotiator for the Ayutook tribe.

When Essence was old enough to marry, she chose a man who interacted well with the colonists. "Warring is not the way to winning," he said. "War brings only death and bloodshed." Charity, he deduced, was the sinew that held civilization together. When charity was lost, all was lost.

Essence's husband became the Ayutook chief, and they learned much about the white man's ways. In time, Essence became a Christian. For years, she prayed for her brother, chief of the Kotopaxis. He was a good man but misguided and wrong-headed in some areas. One of those areas was his demand for annihilation of the weak, the crippled, the permanently injured. He listened to no advice but that of the witch doctor.

As a condition for her cooking her brother's beloved johnnycake, she insisted on the removal of all the scalps he displayed. He would make no other concessions. She knew that only God could change his heart. And He did.

The chieftain married a woman named Lithia. Essence moved into Lithia's former pueblo, and although her brother urged her to remain in the tribe, she no longer felt needed. She did not blend with the women of the tribe, squaws who had their own families and friends. Some of them were jealous of her beauty. She soon returned to her own tribe, the Ayutooks.

A new Ayutook chief had taken over in Essence's absence. He was devoid of leadership qualities, and much had changed. The tribe was still sympathetic to the traders and settlers, but many of them had returned to their heathen worship. They were a mixed multitude, bickering among themselves.

It seemed to Essence that she was a stranger everywhere she went. Since her own losses, Essence had invited the weak, the troubled, and the sickly to rest their cares upon her shoulders. They had done so without discovering that inside this strong, reliable Indian woman there was a crying loneliness. She had no one left, no anchor for her heart. To add to her concern was a rumor that the new government planned to take her land, her home. Except for her trust in God and her solace in the woods, she had nothing.

She wished that she might know more about Jesus. She'd heard that there was a Book that told about Him. Although she had learned to speak the English language fluently, she had not learned to read. Now her brother and his wife, Lithia, were also searching for more knowledge about the true God. Where could they find a teacher?

The old medicine man of the Kotopaxis had died, and the chief had refused to employ another. They had hoped that the white missionary who took refuge in Lithia's pueblo might return, but they had heard nothing more from him—and that had been a year ago.

Essence fell into pensive thought, thought that contributed to her forlornness, as she wandered aimlessly off the trail and through the underbrush. She remembered how she had felt when she lost her husband and her children. Wild with grief, she had wished to die, too, to go with them, but being alive, she had to live. In her time of greatest distress, God spoke to her heart. He showed her that her lost family must live on through her.

What would life have been like had her husband lived? He was a good chief, honest and amiable. The tribe's inner strife would not be raging if he were here. What about her children? Her son would be near manhood now; he would gather firewood for her, bring her winter meat. . . .

She seldom let her mind rove this far as it was too distressing. She missed her husband, but she missed her children more. They had been the joy of her life.

Essence loved Lithia's handicapped son. Victor had come to visit her every day when she lived in the Kotopaxi village. Had she done the right thing by moving away? There, at least, she had the boy. She thought she would be more content among her own people again, but in truth, she found no fulfillment here. She even felt rejection. What should she do?

She gathered her scant knowledge of prayer into her searching mind and asked God for direction. She did not wish to spend a useless life without love and without purpose.

Beyond the river, she heard a crashing in the bushes and supposed it was a bear. She raised her nose and sniffed. The smell wasn't that of a bear; it was the unmistakable scent of a white man.

—

Chapter Nine

Lost Possessions

With the daily closeness of Marianne, Perregrine's urgency to find a parson to make her his wife accelerated. His heart was especially susceptible to the brittle little laugh that came at unexpected times and for unexpected reasons. She was unpredictable, this lassie, but a pleasure to the eyes. He pictured her face in a gilded frame to highlight her hair like a blaze of apricot fire. It would be such a wondrous portrait that one would never tire of the gazing.

Marianne had lost her buttonhook somewhere, and he now fastened her shoes with his one good hand. His attention to this small detail pleased her.

His mind was settled that he could not continue to be a missionary and care for Marianne as well. Someone else would have to play out his religious role; someone else could answer the Kotopaxi chief's plea. There were other men who were better suited than himself. He'd had precious little reward for his labors anyway.

His mother, back in the old country, would be

shocked—and maybe disappointed—that he had chosen a mate so . . . what was the word? *Impractical*—that was it. Marianne would always be improvident and a leaner. But, of course, Marie Abelard would love Marianne. Anyone would. One could not keep from it.

How would Marie act when she learned that Perregrine had given up his work for the Lord? Marie had been proud to have a son who dedicated himself to God's service. She had bent the ear of any and every neighbor with her boasting. That calling was higher than being crowned King of England, she had told Perregrine. Sooner or later, though, she would adjust, Perregrine supposed, to the idea that he had abandoned the call. She would have to.

And Lewis . . . ? Lewis had come all the way across the ocean to support his younger brother's evangelism. *He* wouldn't make the sacrifice, but he gloried in Perregrine's commitment. What would Lewis think of his brother's marriage? He could hear Lewis's good-natured howl now: "Perregrine, you dolt, she is *out of your class.*" Was that Lewis's imaginary voice that spoke, or was it some inner revelation that summoned the thought?

Yes, Marianne *was* of a different world. Her view of religion was limited to belfries and stained-glass windows. She was clueless as to real Christianity. To her, spiritual success was a pretty building and a fine pipe organ. She probably never would change. She rather reminded him of Lewis, accepting life as a giant carnival, living a carefree existence without delving for deeper meanings.

Her sweet whine brought him back to the present. "I am weary with the trees, dear Perry," she sighed. "Please, let's find people. I need to see people, to talk to people, to be with people."

"I am here, Marianne."

"But you are only one. I am crowd hungry. Can't we

go faster?" She was able to limp along now, supporting part of her weight on his arm. "How much further is it to a town?"

"I wish I knew, my dear child," he said, thinking how true the word "child" rang. "But I don't even know where we are. Eventually we will find a habitation, but you must be patient."

"I think I shall *die* if I have to eat one more nasty fish!" she pouted. "Please find me something fit to eat."

"If it were spring, there would be plenty of fresh vegetation, but with winter coming on—"

"All I can think of is the ices and the cakes at the dinner parties. Can't you just taste them now, Perry?"

He remembered his mother's gingerbread. "Yes," he said.

When he found some early winter grapes, leathery to bite into but sweet and tangy past their skins, Marianne was as delighted as a little girl with a toy. Her moods rose and fell with the present and how it pleased her. One disagreeable moment could unravel her whole day, but just as easily, a pleasant incident could sew up her fragmented hopes.

She seldom mentioned her deceased aunt; grief hadn't a place to lodge for long in the fiber of her being. That trait, Perregrine decided, was to her advantage.

"And when we are married, I will never have to tramp through the horrible woods again, or eat fish, or sleep on a sled, will I, Perry?"

"I should hope not, dear."

"Just think, Perry," she was off on another fantasy trip. "We shall have a wonderful wedding with guests and flowers and yards of lace."

A nagging worry assailed Perregrine, quelling his response. He was penniless. How would he find a dime to pay a parson for the simplest ceremony, let alone a gallant affair such as Marianne wished and deserved?

"I'm afraid I haven't the funds for a public ceremony, Marianne. We will be united in private by the first preacher we meet. That will have to do."

"What?" Her face puckered, and he saw that she was about to cry. "There will be no pretty wedding dress for me?"

How could he explain his circumstances to her, a stranger to poverty? He had been traveling these two years in America, asking for no donations, receiving no remuneration. Lewis had a profitable job, and he might lend Perregrine the money for the sort of wedding Marianne wished, but Perregrine shrank from the thought of begging for money. Hadn't the Lord promised to supply his needs?

"You didn't answer me about the dress, Perry," she prodded.

"I . . . I'm afraid I haven't the money for a fancy dress."

The tinkly laugh came again, catching Perregrine off guard. He had thought she was ready to weep, and instead she laughed. "Silly Perry, there is enough money in Aunt Eleanor's handbag for a hundred dresses!"

"But we must return her money to her husband, your uncle."

"It wasn't his money. It was Aunt Eleanor's money. And mine. My mother and father left a large estate. They would wish me to have a proper wedding. I would not want to disappoint them."

Then the Lord had supplied.

"As you wish, pretty Marianne."

She responded to his compliment like a flower in the sun. "I like for you to say I'm pretty."

"The truth never hurt anybody."

"In the forest, I don't feel pretty, Perry. My clothes

are all rumpled, and my hair is not properly crimped. Just wait until you see me in the city. You will think me stunning!"

"If you pretty up any more, I don't know if my old heart can bear it," teased Perregrine.

A bird scolded in a nearby tree, causing Perregrine to stand rooted in his tracks. Someone was coming. Or was it an animal? He signaled for Marianne to be silent.

As the minor notes of a song floated across the river, Perregrine pulled Marianne into a clump of low shrubs, leaving the trunk on the sled. He hadn't time to rescue both it and her.

A pretty Indian woman came down the trail to the river's edge and sat down on a rock. Her blue-black braid glistened in the afternoon sun. She fingered the fringes on her sleeve, straightening them. Then she raised her nose in the air and sniffed, sensing that someone was near. She scrutinized the landscape to locate a possible enemy.

Marianne would have screamed had not Perregrine clamped a hand over her mouth. "Shhh," he hissed in her ear. "Indians." She went into a swoon.

The Indian woman spotted the wooden sled. She removed her moccasins and waded across the stream to examine it. With open curiosity, she poked at the portmanteau. Then she pushed the contraption to the bank of the river to take it back across with her.

Perregrine was at a loss to know what to do. If he showed himself and she was a member of an enemy tribe, he would have the entire regiment of warriors on his neck. He could not risk Marianne's life. Yet if he allowed the woman to take the luggage, Marianne would have nothing for the remainder of the journey. He weighed his options and decided that her life was of more value than her clothing or their money.

The river's current caught the sled and spun it about crazily before sending it headlong downstream. Unsuccessfully, the woman grappled for it then watched it plummet away.

By the time the Indian had retreated back up the trail from which she had come, Marianne had revived, and tears dropped from her chin. She was staring at the vacant spot where the sled had been.

"Oh, my trunk is gone!" she sobbed. "My clothes, my money, *everything* is gone! What is life without *things*? Now I am without a change of garments, and I shall be uglier. I wish that I had died with Aunt Eleanor! Pray tell, Perry, whatever shall we do now?"

The seriousness of their situation dismayed him. The extra clothes for their bedding and protection against the elements were gone. "Marianne, we have no choice. You must sit here quietly while I follow the trail that swallowed that Indian squaw. Now that we have no resources, we must have humanity, whatever the race. We will need blankets and clothing. I will bargain with the Indian tribe."

"No, no! Don't leave me! They might kill you, and then I would be here alone for the bears to eat!"

"I am not afraid for myself, but I can't chance putting you in danger."

"If you leave me here, I shall die of fright anyway." She clung to his arm and would not let go.

"Then come along. We will go together, for better or for worse. We haven't much more to lose, have we?"

"The wedding, Perry," she reminded at this inopportune time. "What shall we do for a proper wedding now that Aunt Eleanor's purse is gone?" The present predicament was devoured by the threat to her future dream.

Keep her happy, Perregrine. Keep her mind off the crisis at hand.

From his pocket he pulled the rings and the brooch he had removed from the body of Eleanor English. "We can sell these. They are quite valuable, are they not?"

"Oh, you dear, dear man!" she exclaimed. She flung her arms about his neck and hugged him exuberantly, completely disorienting him. "I shall have a proper wedding after all! You think of everything. You shall make a marvelous husband! We shall be mad with happiness, living for nothing but music and games and fun!"

Perregrine's smile was a frozen ache that he could not allow to melt. With his one good arm, he carried her across the river so that her feet would not get wet.

Chapter Ten

The Dream

Robin awoke in a panic, not knowing where she was. She'd had the dream again, and her pillow was damp with tears. It was always the same, this tormenting dream.

Opening her eyes, she puzzled over the clean, white walls graced with paintings. Where was her rag bed, her broken cup? Why were her much darned black stockings hanging on the back of that nice chair? Then she remembered, and the tide of her fear ebbed. She was in Lewis Abelard's apartment. Hers was the bed with the high, carved headboard on which cupids tugged at a wreath of roses. *And I have no right to be here,* she thought.

Marie heard her stirring about and called, "You must show me the way to market today, Robin. My Lewis does not know what groceries to buy. He has no saleratus and no flavorings and no flour for flapjacks. Men know nothing about cooking. I have a list as long as my arm. We must have nourishment!"

Distractedly, the girl dressed, saying nothing. It had

been several months since the dream had come to taunt her; she had hoped that she might be done with it forever.

When she walked into the kitchen, Marie studied her face with motherly concern. It wasn't the same tranquil face Robin had worn the day before. "You did not rest well?" she asked solicitously.

"I am resting well, but I am dreaming bad, thanks, mem," Robin said, her eyes washed with weariness. "But I will be marketing with thee. I will then be cleaning today only once."

"Your eyes are sad."

"Yes, mem. The dreaming is in my head."

"You had a very bad dream?"

"Always I am dreaming the same."

Marie's nurturing instinct flared into sympathy for the woebegone girl. "Would you like to tell me about it?"

"I have never been telling it."

"If you had rather not—"

Robin gave a tired sigh. "If I am telling thee, I am hoping it to go away. Always I am dreaming about the ocean and the going boat. I am a small girl then. I go and go. So longing. Then the splintering of the boat is coming. I am trying to scream, but I am not making a sound. The water is taking mine away on the board floating and floating. Very far. So long I am floating in the cold waters. I am holding on the boarding tight. Other is with mine floating, too, but other is lost. Mine mema is lost and mine pepa.

"A shore man is rescuing. He is pulling on mine from the cold water. He is a big man and white with beard on his face. Very old. He is seeing the lost other and is sad. But mine mema and pepa he is not finding. He is calling mine name Robin because I look much like a soaking bird, he is saying.

"The man is taking me to a logging house where is living a new Quaker mema. She is saying she will be taking mine and taking the care always. The old man is saying much thank you.

"She is loving mine, the Quaker mema, but she is dying and leaving mine again with no mema." Robin shrugged her small shoulders and held out her palms, upturned. "Always I am dreaming the same. I am thinking: Is it a dreaming or a remembering?" She pointed to her head.

"You mean you think this may have really happened, and you are reminded of it by the dream?" Marie asked.

"I am thinking, maybe yes, maybe no. The Quaker mema only I am knowing is true."

Robin looked so dismal that Marie's compassion went out to her. She hurried to the girl and put her arms about her. When she did, Robin broke into hard, shuddering sobs.

"I am sorry, Robin," Marie consoled. "I wish I could erase the dream." She patted Robin's shoulder. "Can I do anything to make you feel better?"

Robin only wept harder.

"Please don't cry, dear child."

"I am not crying for the dreaming," gulped Robin between sniffles.

"Then why do you cry?"

"It is the first time that anybody is touching mine since mine mema Quaker died. No hands are feeling on mine shoulder. No arms are tender. Thy care is crying mine heart so beautiful, mem."

Marie hugged the girl to herself and let her shed the pent-up tears. When the emotional storm abated, she asked, "Where did you go when your Quaker mother died?"

"Only to the streets to be working."

"How old are you?"

"Mine age I am not knowing. Mine Quaker mema is

thinking I am maybe three, maybe four when she is first a mema for mine. For only ten years, she has mine, then she is going. After that, I am working."

"Your Quaker mother had other children."

"Eight children in all. All are loving by mema, and she is treating mine like a daughter. But all the others are boys."

"What was the name? The surname?"

"The sir's name? Mine pepa?"

"The family name."

"Smyth. It is a common name, yes? Many names of Smyth is in Philadelphia and everywhere."

"Why didn't you stay with your adopted family when your Quaker mother died?"

Robin bit her lower lip and ducked her head. "The one older boy is naming Theodore. He is wanting to marriage mine. I am not readying to marry. I am not even knowing how old I am, but I am too childish yet. Thou art understanding?"

"Yes, I understand."

Robin looked up, a sort of defiance in her eyes. "So I am running away to be living for mine self. It is not easy to get food. Or a place to be sleeping. But I am finding work with a few pennies. And I am keeping mine self . . . pure."

"I am proud of you, Robin. How long have you worked?"

"I am thinking six years now."

"So you would be about twenty?"

"I am so thinking. It is sad not knowing who one is or how old."

"Did your Quaker mother send you to school?"

"She is teaching me at home. The reading and the writing, it is hard for me. I am thinking I was not knowing the English language. I am wondering where is mine home country. If the boat is crashing mine, where am I coming from to this landing in America? I am too small then to remember."

"You remember nothing of your father or mother on the ship?"

"Nothing except the dreams."

"You do not remember the language your parents spoke?"

"Not a word. If maybe I am hearing it, I would. Oh, I am wishing!"

"We will make it a matter of prayer, Robin. Do you know how to pray?"

"Oh, yes, mem. I am knowing only my Quaker mema's praying. It is good?"

"All prayer to God is good. I will pray with you."

"Thank you, mem."

They knelt and prayed. After a simple breakfast, they went to the general store, where Marie purchased a generous supply of staples. On a whim, she splurged and bought a bag of horehound candy for Robin. Her boys had always enjoyed sweet surprises.

"Do you like gingerbread cakes?" she asked Robin.

"They are not knowing to mine," Robin said. "What are they tasting?"

"They have a sugary frosting and are wonderful with tea! I will make some for you."

"Thou must not be tiring thyself to cooking for mine, mem."

"I like to bake cakes. My Lewis especially likes gingerbread, and so does Perregrine."

"I shall be delighting to try thine cakes. And I can be learning maybe to cook the cakes mine self?" Her eyes glowed with interest. "Thou wouldst be teaching mine the cooking?" Then the same eyes clouded. "But I am maybe too hard to learn."

"The cakes are simple. I will show you."

As they approached Elfreth's Court, Margot was just leaving Lewis's front door. There was no place for Marie to hide to avoid a confrontation.

"Oh, Mrs. Abelahd," she babbled when she saw the bundle-bearing woman. "I came to see if Lewis maht have retuhned today."

"Not yet," chirped Marie, "but we are having a grand time during the wait, Robin and I. My, I don't know what I would do without Robin! I am sure God sent her to me. She has been like an angel from heaven, staying the night with me, showing me to the store, and we're even going to make cakes!"

Margot scowled.

"You will come in for a visit?" invited Marie.

"No, not until Lewis retuhns." Her words had an edge that Marie did not miss. "Good day, Mrs. Abelahd." She turned and marched off with her back straight as a ridge pole.

"Now what ruffled her *feathahs*?" Marie mused, her Margot mimicry so perfect it brought a giggle from Robin.

"She is not liking mine, I am thinking," Robin said. "She is looking mean at mine."

"Don't let it *bothah* you," Marie advised, perversely enjoying the impersonation.

"No, mem. I am not letting it bother mine. You are mine friend, and that is all that is mattering."

Inside the apartment, Robin helped Marie arrange the groceries in the pantry. They chatted and laughed, becoming more and more comfortable with each other.

"I must be working now," Robin announced when the supplies were stowed. "Only I am cleaning one today. No more."

"May I go with you and help?"

"Oh, no, mem! I am always jobbing by mine self. I am strong and young. Thou art—" she started to say old, but changed her mind, "—not so strong." She hurried away but not before impulsively throwing her arms around Marie. "Thou art so mothering. I am loving thee more forever!" she bubbled with joy.

And then she was gone.

Chapter Eleven

Encounter

The dream was forgotten in Robin's newfound happiness. She worked with a will, longing to return to Marie, for Marie had said that Robin should have her first lesson in gingerbread making today.

Robin's work assignment was in Elfreth's Court; she rejoiced that Marie was not far away. Her return would require but a short walking distance. "Thank Thee, Father God, for Mr. Lewis's sweet mema," she whispered. "And for the soft bed with no wharf rats. And for the food I am never tasting before. Thank Thee that I am having someone to be loving mine again."

Lewis would return soon, and he would blot up most of his mother's attention. However, Robin planned to sop the leftover batter from the bowl of Marie's affection after Lewis had taken his fill. Of course, she would return to the dirt floor of the old storage room in the warehouse. But she would have a friend, and that's what mattered.

"Your eyes have a new light today," mentioned the

woman for whom she cleaned. She pulled her new baby to her breast. "It makes you . . . prettier."

"Mine eyes, they are shining?" The glimmer of a smile passed over Robin's lips. "It is because I am having a new friend."

"You are courting?"

"Courting? What is that meaning—courting?"

"Your new friend is a man?"

"Oh, no, mem! A mothering lady from the faraway ocean is asking mine to be staying with her and being her friend."

"It is not your mother?"

"Only I am wishing that she is being mine mema."

"I see. But you will still work for me until I am strong again? I don't think that I can manage the baby—"

"Oh, yes, mem. Still I am working always. My friend is living here at the Elfreth's. It is the Mrs. Abelard."

"Lewis Abelard's mother."

"Yes, mem."

Robin moved to the next room, but as she left, she gave one yearning glance at the child cradled safely in his mother's arms. Once she was thus held. She would give anything to know the woman—forever gone—who had sung lullabies to her.

Two hours later, with her work finished, Robin stepped out into the brisk air to return to Lewis's apartment. Marie would be waiting with the wonderful recipe for the cake. . . .

Margot Payne blocked Robin's path. Robin stepped aside to go around her.

"I need to talk to you befoah you go any fuhthah." Margot's eyes narrowed and pierced.

"Yes?" Robin looked full into Margot's wrathful face. She saw no reason to be intimidated by paint and powder.

84

"Lewis has hiahed you as his housekeepah, raht?"

"I am cleaning work for him, yes, mem."

"You do know who I am, don't you?"

"I am never meeting thee before I am coming from the shopping with Lewis's mema today."

"Such dreadful English! People who cannot speak propahly should nevah come to America! And all suhvants should be requiahed to study language! I certainly wouldn't have you as my housekeepah!"

"I should not be working for thee if thou wouldst be asking, mem," Robin stated simply.

"You *would*, you impudent paupah!" barked Margot. "It would be discrimination if you preferred othahs above me!"

"If thou wilt please not be asking. I shall saying no to thee. I am filling mine days with working already."

"And do you know to whom you are speaking? Your futuah employah! I shall soon be married to Lewis Abelahd, and you shall scrub my floahs!"

"Mr. Abelard will be telling mine what to be doing, please." Robin tried to move on, but again Margot became a barrier to her freedom.

"I am not finished, you little vixen. I know what you are trahing to do. I know your kind. You are trahing to buttah up to my futuah mothah-in-law."

"I am—"

"You have no business spending the night in Lewis's nice apahtment."

Faint lines of perplexity wrinkled Robin's forehead. "The Mrs. Abelard is asking me."

"She asked you out of courtesy. That is the custom of English gentry. You should have ansahed no."

"I am doing that, but—"

"You are lying! You want to get on the good side of Lewis's mothah and maybe try to steal Lewis from me.

85

But I'm wahning you, it won't work!"

"No! It is never in the thinking!"

"Whatevah you're thinking, you could nevah do it! Lewis loves me devotedly. And since we are engaged to be married, I shall demand that you not retuhn to his apahtment until it is again time to clean next week."

"The mem is looking for mine now so that we are making the cakes."

"I will tell her you ah not returning. It is against the rules of the management for othahs to stay in the rooms without pay. Mrs. Abelahd does not know the rules. I shall repoaht you at once if you return. It will make much bothah for Lewis."

"But his mema is there staying."

"She is a blood relative. Only relatives can be house guests. Are you related to the Abelahds?"

"No, but—"

"Then make yourself scarce. There are no exceptions to the rules. You will be asked to leave by the proprietah if you go back. I will watch and send someone to expel you at once. It will be most embarrassing for you. Mrs. Abelahd would nevah have invited you to stay with her had she known the law."

"She will be wondering why I am not returning."

"I told you that I would explain to Mrs. Abelahd. She is intelligent enough to undahstand, I am sure."

Robin did not want to cause problems for her new friend, a friend who was as ignorant of the Elfreth housing regulations as she was. So she turned and with downcast eyes walked back toward the warehouse on the seashore.

She went inside the building, but today the windowless prison couldn't hold her. She plodded down to the jetty and sat on a graying beam where she could watch the waves rush up the sloping beach of purple and black pebbles. It was cold, and she shivered from the breath of the breakers. She sorely missed Marie's laughter, her nearness. The day, welcomed with such joy, was bitter in her mouth. It would be a week before she saw her friend again.

Robin's eyes scanned the horizon until she found a ship, only a speck in the distance. A column of smoke billowed from its smokestack. Was it on such a vessel that her mother and father sailed to America? Were there brothers and sisters? Some niggling memory told her that she was not the only child set adrift. What happened to the others? Could it be that she was separated from her siblings and that some of them had survived also?

If only she could remember her name!

Chapter Twelve

Cold Trail

Lewis found the scattered remains of the coach and three shallow graves, but the hastily planted wooden crosses gave no hint as to the identity of the casualties.

Lewis felt a sickening wave of fear. It was new and it was awful, the dryness of his mouth, the prickling of his skin. Did his brother, Perregrine, lie beneath one of those mounds of earth? He had to know. *My brother, Perregrine . . .*

Falling to his knees, he began to dig at the ground with his bare hands. *What shall I tell our mother, Perregrine, if I have failed you? I promised her that I would be your guardian on this wild and dangerous frontier.*

The first body that Lewis unearthed was that of Eleanor English, still bedecked in her ridiculous hat. He quickly put her back to rest beneath her curtain of dust, a third of his fears lopped off. According to the statesman, there were two female passengers and two male passengers on the ill-fated coach. One man and one woman got away. Likely the driver escaped.

The next grave Lewis clawed through produced a man's booted foot. It could belong to Perregrine, or as easily it could not. Sweat dripped from Lewis's face even though the weather was pleasantly cool; suspense tied knots in his stomach. With no shovel, his progress was agonizingly slow. But when he uncovered the head, he saw by the sparse hair that it was not Perregrine. Had he harbored doubts, they would have been dispelled when he noticed the empty liquor bottle that lay beneath the shroud. Two-thirds of Lewis's worries were blotted out.

With hands raw from digging and fingernails caked with black soil, Lewis's pace slackened. Not only was he tired, he was afraid of what the last cross would reveal. He wanted to know yet dreaded the knowledge. However, the dead driver bore no resemblance to Perregrine, and the two good hands he unveiled left his mind at rest. Somewhere Perregrine was alive, running for his life. Lewis wept glad tears, and his guilt lifted. Even if his brother had been wounded, the injury must not have been significant because there were no clues of a struggle.

Perregrine would follow the water; that had always been his strategy. Lewis set out in the direction his brother most surely headed: east. Perregrine would try to get back to civilization, back to the city.

Lewis was encouraged by signs of recent camps here and there: a fire pit, a discarded drinking gourd, a bed of leaves. He followed the tracks of the sled. Farther on, he came to a cave and found the remains of a charred wooden arm with only a finger unburned. He had carved that arm for Perregrine himself. Yes, his brother was alive and able to care for himself, able to build fires. The instinct for survival was strong in him.

A buttonhook lay near the cave's mouth. On the handle were the initials "M. E." The surviving woman must be with him. Lewis's mouth twisted into a comical smirk when he thought of Perregrine with his female freight. Women terrified Perregrine. Still grinning, Lewis dropped the buttonhook into his pocket.

No friend of the outdoors, Lewis doggedly followed the stream in search of Perregrine. He loathed sleeping on the ground and longed for the comforts of a feather bed. How long would it take to find Perregrine? Or was it even necessary to continue the seeking now that he knew Perregrine had escaped?

Then Lewis came to the place where the sled had been launched into the river. He crossed to the other side, finding no signs that Perregrine had taken to the land again. *He'll show up sooner or later,* Lewis allowed in his sanguine mind. *I know that he survived, and that is what matters.* He had been on the trail for a fortnight and had his fill of land without luxuries; he was ready to return to a more exciting life. With his worries muted, he set his course back toward Philadelphia.

In the city, Marie had turned Margot Payne from her door on a daily basis, and as Lewis rounded the corner to Elfreth's Court, she was shooing the socialite away once again. Lewis stepped back into the shadows to await Margot's departure, puzzled and confused. Who had answered the door of his apartment? It wasn't Robin; it was an older woman. Surely the manager hadn't let his rooms out to someone else in his short absence! His rent was well paid in advance. But just in case the unthinkable had happened, it might behoove him to use the door clapper instead of his key. He wouldn't want to walk in on a stranger.

Marie answered the knock, expecting another unpleasant encounter with Margot. A frown dominated her face. "I told you—" she began and bit the rebuke off with a squeal of delight. "Lewis! Welcome home!"

Nothing made sense to Lewis. This woman with sedge-colored hair looked very much like his own mother. But, of course, it couldn't be. His mother was thousands of miles away, across the ocean, making gingerbread and filling her vases with dried clover from the glen.

"Lewis!" she scolded in motherly fashion. "Are you just going to stand there? Haven't you a hug for your mother?"

He rubbed his eyes. "My *mother?*"

"Yes, I am still your mother. Marie Elizabeth Abelard. Don't you remember me?"

The irony of the situation pulled Lewis back to his jovial self. "You do look familiar." He folded her into his arms. "But haven't you strayed from your yard?"

"I have come to your house to play," she quipped, "and to pray. I will be partly like you and partly like Perregrine. But how did you find our Perregrine?"

"I didn't—"

She grabbed his arm. "Perregrine is *gone?*"

"No, mother. No more 'gone' than usual. He is wandering in the woods somewhere among his uncivilized friends. I found where he had been. I'm sure we will be hearing from him soon. But I can't keep the boy in arms. The first one I carved for him he gave to a handless child who needed it. Now, I find that he has used the second for *firewood*. I might make a profit if I didn't have to spend all my time carving prosthesis for an irresponsible brother!"

"If anyone else used such an objectionable adjective for your brother, you would cuff him."

"That I would."

"I have come to see after both of you, Lewis."

"You are welcome, and I am delighted that you are here, Mother, but it wasn't necessary for you to make such a long journey. I am doing a commendable job of taking care of myself."

"I know it, Lewis, I know it. My mother heart was just lonesome. What did I have to live for there when my two boys were here?"

"That is a sound argument, Mother. The reasoning is distinctly Marie Abelard, the world's most son-spoiling matriarch."

"But, please, Lewis, if we may find Robin to stay with me and help me in the house—"

"Robin?"

"Your beautiful little housekeeper. She found me sitting on your doorstep and never stopped fussing over me until she had me comfortably settled in your apartment here. Then she went to work and did not return."

"As you say, dear mother. Now that you've come, it is my responsibility to please you."

"And another thing. There's a horrible girl who calls every day. She has become an abominable pest. She is painted up like a jester, and her fingers look like they are dripping blood. And her lips—"

"You are speaking of the girl you sent away just before I came?"

"You saw her?"

"Yes."

"Lewis, she's—she's—"

"She is Margot Payne, and she is rightly named. She is a pain."

"But she says that she is engaged to be married."

"To whom?"

"To you."

"To *me*?"

"And soon, she claims."

"You can't believe half you hear in Philadelphia, Mother. It is wishful thinking on her part. I have given her no reason to draw such a conclusion. Give it no thought."

"It is a scandal, her boldness. Are all girls in America so . . . so forward?"

"Not all of them, but times have changed. Women are less inhibited in this new land. They like to think of themselves as liberated."

"Times may change, but *ladies* never change."

He hugged her. "Rightly said. When I find a lady like you, I shall weaken my resolve never to wed!"

"Oh, but you must marry, Lewis! I must have a daughter-in-law. I brought the Bible to write in the 'who' and the 'when.' But mind you, she must be the right one and not that dreadful Margot Payne!"

Chapter Thirteen

The Ayutooks

"You trade?" Believing Perregrine to be a barterer, the Ayutook chief who spoke little English sent him to Essence.

Perregrine introduced himself and Marianne, weak with relief that they had fallen into the hands of a friendly tribe. God had directed their path.

Marianne remained mute and pale. Her eyes darted about in alarm. She didn't like the dark and strangely dressed people about her; they were Indians, and all Indians were evil. She hoped that she and Perregrine could buy a horse and blankets from these savages and be on their way before sundown. Marianne had never ridden a horse, and this gave her a qualm, but she figured she could cling to Perregrine as he managed the reins. Anything to get them back to a populated place, back to the paradise of the city!

Essence was kind and soft-spoken, and Perregrine liked her. "You are lost?" she asked.

"We have been traveling for many days."

"Then you must be tired and hungry. I will prepare food for you in my teepee. I have fresh venison. The hunt went well this year. Our Heavenly Father was good to us."

Perregrine's face lighted with joy. "You are a Christian?"

"Yes, I am a Christian."

Soon they were conversing like old friends. Perregrine, open to her camaraderie, told Essence of the ambush and of Marianne's injuries. Marianne buried her head in her hands, wishing only to flee. Assuming Marianne's actions sprung from grief, Essence reached out to comfort the girl. But Marianne drew back.

"She is frightened," explained Perregrine, hoping that Essence would understand.

"She will lose her fears," Essence smiled. "Our tribe is no threat. We are a brotherly tribe. Both of you may stay with me as long as you wish. No harm will come to you."

"Marianne will want to go on as soon as possible. We have lost our luggage and will need to borrow some supplies."

"What is luggage?"

"The box that held Marianne's clothing. We pulled it along behind us on a wooden raft."

Essence's mouth flew open. "Oh, I am afraid that I am to blame!" she blurted. "I found the box on the creek bank and tried to rescue it. We have many traders. Instead, the whole raft slipped away down the rapids. I am so sorry!"

Perregrine found himself chuckling at her ruefulness. "We were watching from behind the brush."

"You were? Why didn't you stop me?"

"Marianne was afraid. She has been through much. I didn't want to expose her to more harm. Some tribes are not friendly."

Essence nodded soberly. "Unfortunately, you are right. Again, I offer my apologies. The box flew down the river from the grip of my hands while the river laughed at me."

"We will manage without it."

"But you surely must rest a few days before you go on your long journey. Essence will care for you well. The girl needs a long sleep."

Marianne's face wore petulance.

Perregrine spoke up. "And I, myself, am very fatigued from the worry of saving Marianne's life. I will need a peaceful night's rest before I am able to travel again."

"Of course. And much nourishing food. I have some fish—"

Marianne opened her mouth to speak, but Perregrine hastily intercepted her remark. "I'm afraid Marianne has eaten so much fish it now makes her sick."

"I am sorry. Then I will cook something else. We will please the young lady. I have soft elk-skin beds. And I will give Marianne fresh clothes."

Marianne looked at Essence's dress and shook her head. She would accept no Indian garb.

"Only while I wash yours for you, pretty golden-haired girl," Essence said. "Then you will have your beautiful dress back." Perregrine deemed Essence a paragon of wisdom, handling Marianne with a woman's intuition. His burden suddenly felt lighter, and he sent up an unspoken thanks.

While they were talking, two traders arrived. Essence introduced them as Abe King and Theodore Smyth. The traders had heard of the massacre and were anxious to hear the details. They made conversation with Perregrine, and when Perregrine learned that they took their furs to a trading post in Philadelphia, he asked them to deliver a message to his brother, Lewis. He needed to let Lewis know where he was and that he was safe. Mr. King knew the location of Elfreth's Court, and Mr. Smyth added, "We will be glad to oblige thee, sir." Neither of the men were successful in averting their eyes from Marianne.

Essence served a tasty stew to her visitors, and even Marianne seemed to relax and enjoy the meal. Now and then she smiled. Yet when the traders departed, she acted restless again.

Essence took a stone jar to the spring for fresh water for Marianne's bath.

"You are not feeling well?" Perregrine asked when Essence had gone.

"I do not like these people, and I do not want to stay here even one night," she whimpered. "The tent *smells*, and I dislike smells."

"This is a very kind squaw," pointed out Perregrine. "She treats you with great care. You will have a warm and comfortable bed tonight."

"I will not sleep a whit."

"We must not rush away; that would be impolite. It would say that we do not appreciate the tribe's hospitality. If we show no gratitude, I might not be able to negotiate for a horse. Besides, I need rest. My chest grows heavy from the cold and dampness of the trail. You must not be ungrateful, Marianne, and you must have fortitude."

It was the first time Perregrine had been firm with her, and Marianne resented his words. She started to sulk.

"You must grow up," he added without diplomacy, "for you will soon be a wife and no longer a pampered child. It would behoove you to learn to take temporary inconveniences for what they are."

"I will not live with you in these woods!"

"I am not asking that of you. I am only asking that

you be reasonable and try to accept what we can do nothing about until we can get ourselves back to the city." His voice softened. "Then I will do everything possible to make your life cheerful and happy, dear."

A small smile twitched at her mouth. "Thank you, Perregrine." It was the first time she had used his full name, and it made her sound mature. "Today, I will do my best with things I am not accustomed to."

"That's a brave lady!"

Suddenly, she found herself glad that she had made him proud of her. It was a good feeling. "Under the proper circumstances, I will be a very good wife, Perregrine," she said. "I have been well bred. You have not yet had the pleasure of seeing the finer side of me. In society, I perform well. My father sent me to a finishing school."

"I don't doubt that you will be a perfect mate, dear. I understand that you have been thrown into the most extraordinary of conditions. No lady of your standing could have done better, I am sure." Perregrine was glad for the small altercation. It proved they could compromise, working out their problems together.

As the day dimmed, Essence built up the fire. It tinged the teepee with a suffused glow and brought an unequivocal peace to Perregrine's heart. He reveled in the beauty, the rawness, the love and the life of the wilderness. *This is my world.* A regret struck at some inner fidelity, still tender. *A world I will soon be leaving forever.*

Essence was talking, pulling him from his rumination. "I will ask you what has been your occupation," she said. "A trader?"

"I am a missionary."

"Oh, Mr. Abelard! I cannot tell you how glad I am to hear this! My brother has sought a Christian missionary for a year. He has a gospel-eager heart—"

"Perry will no longer be a missionary," spoke up Marianne flatly. "He will marry me and take care of me when we arrive back in Philadelphia. This is what he promised." It was the first time Marianne had spoken directly to Essence.

"You will no longer be a Christian, Mr. Abelard?" Essence asked, misunderstanding.

Perregrine dropped his eyes. "Oh, yes, I will live a Christian life, but I will no longer travel to the various tribes—"

"Then who will do that for God, Mr. Abelard? Who will take your place?"

Perregrine squirmed. "I . . . I don't know."

"I am sad to hear this," Essence said, tears in her voice. "My brother and his tribe are in pitiful need of God's teachings and guidance. He was a very hard man and an arrogant one, my brother was. He once had a rule to destroy all the weak and sick and crippled. He also warred against the white man and took scalps.

"Then a strange thing happened. A white missionary who had escaped his arrow took shelter in the pueblo of a woman in his tribe. He told her about God's love—"

Perregrine leaned forward so eagerly that Marianne pulled at his sleeve. She didn't want him engrossed in tales of missionaries. "Tell me about it. What happened?" Perregrine pressed.

"Lithia—that was the squaw's name—and her son were facing death the next day at the hands of my brother. But when my brother came for them, a huge rattlesnake struck at him. Lithia's son, whom she called Broken Bow, flung himself between the viper and my brother. The snake struck the boy's hand, but it was made of wood. The missionary had given the boy his own hand—"

Essence's sentence slid to a stop as Perregrine

100

motioned to his stub of an arm. "It . . . it was *you*, wasn't it?" she gasped. "You were that missionary."

"What was the name of the tribe?"

"The Kotopaxis."

Perregrine's world swam. "Y-yes. I was that missionary."

"My brother married Lithia and adopted her son as his own. They have been looking for you ever since. They want you to come back and tell them more about Jesus."

Chapter Fourteen

Illness

Marianne felt an urgency to get Perregrine away from Essence. All the Indian woman wanted to talk about was missionary work and her brother who needed a Christian teacher. Marianne harbored a flutter of fear that Essence might influence Perregrine, drawing him back to his old calling. She couldn't let that happen.

She started wheedling the next morning. "I am feeling rested and ready to travel, Perregrine," she hinted. (Lately, when she wanted to make her point, she called him Perregrine.)

"One more day, my Marianne," he pleaded. Shivering spasms shook him every few minutes, but he did his best to hide his weakness from her. "I am just a bit strung out from the journey. My head aches with a fury this morning. Essence is arranging for us to have a good horse; tomorrow will be the day we shall leave."

However, by the third day, a fever raged through Perregrine's body, and he was not able to raise himself from the elk-skin cot. His eyes had no wish to open; his body was content to rest where it was. To make plans for another day would call for insufferable effort. Sometimes he heard sounds coming from a long way off. He listened dreamily, awake inside but asleep on the surface. Or was it the other way around? A voice that uttered fragments seemed beyond a high, thick wall. Was it Marianne's voice?

"*Perregrine!* You must throw off the sickness at once so that we can go on," demanded Marianne as if Perregrine had invited the sickness and could dismiss it at will. Her attitude reeked with impatience.

"We will go. I will take . . . you with me . . . my beautiful . . . Marianne. We will go . . . far away. . . ." Perregrine stared at her through eyes dilated with pain. The unfocused gaze and the halting words made her uneasy and somehow angry.

"I will give him some willow tea to quench his fever," Essence said, misconstruing Marianne's anger for anxiety. "He will be well soon. You will help me to care for the man who will be your husband."

It was real fear that invaded Marianne's eyes then. "I know nothing about caring for the ill," she said.

"I can teach you."

"In the cities we have doctors and nurses and rest houses for the sick." Marianne detested illness. Her sundial only recorded brightness and health. "I'm afraid that you will be obliged to care for both of us. How long do you think the illness will last?"

"I cannot say."

"By all means, we must travel tomorrow."

Essence sat up all that day and then the night. The next morning she awoke Marianne.

"He is better?" the girl inquired.

"No, he is very bad. His eyes no longer know what they are seeing. He coughs blood. It may be a killing sickness, and if he endures for a long while, I cannot sit with him both day and night. I will watch at night, which is the worst time, and you can attend him in the daytime while I sleep."

"No, no! I do not wish to watch. You will please call someone else, someone from your tribe to help. I will pay." Marianne was persuaded that money could do anything, buy anything, solve anything.

"Many of the squaws fear the white man's diseases."

"What he has is contagious?" Unconsciously, Marianne moved back from the cot, putting more distance between herself and the feverish man who did not seem aware of his surroundings.

"This I do not know."

"If there is a possibility, I must stay away. I am susceptible to germs. My mother and father were lost at sea. My aunt has been murdered. I cannot die, too. Then there would be no one to handle the inheritance."

"Then I shall care for him as best I can."

"Please. And I shall see that you are well paid."

"I want no pay. I am glad to attend God's servant. I will sleep only when necessity demands it."

Marianne bit at her top lip. "I do hope that Perry recovers quickly so that we can move on. I wouldn't want to spend the winter here with so little accommodations."

"We will have a mild winter. The animals are putting on thin coats this year. The days that one cannot travel will be but few. You must not worry about it."

Perregrine did not improve. He grew worse until he clung to life by a mere thread. Essence seldom left his side for anything, leaving Marianne without the personal catering she expected. The girl sat with folded hands and internal fumings but doing nothing. It irked her to have to ladle out her own soup.

"I think that the missionary is not going to make it," Essence said at last. "He is too weak."

"What shall *I* do?"

"Since you have no home, I suppose that you could live with me. I could teach you to weave and scrape hides. It is not a bad life."

"Oh, no!" Terror filled Marianne's voice and spread over her face. "I must return to Philadelphia. I have an uncle there. But how shall I find the way?"

"The white traders could show you the way. They come and go often. I should not know how safe or proper it would be for a lady to travel with lone men, however."

"I would not be afraid." The idea appealed to Marianne, but any chance to escape would have gratified her as well. "When they come next, I will go with them."

"Surely you will stay with your future husband until he draws his last breath?"

"I cannot bear to see him die."

"Where shall I bury him?"

"Anywhere."

"We have our own burying grounds—"

"Perregrine wouldn't mind being buried with your people."

"I should think that if you love this man you would wish to stay with him until . . . the end. When my husband was mortally wounded, I treasured every minute of his breath to the last."

"No, I—"

"Miss Marianne, I think you do not love this man." Essence was kind but direct. "You do not love anyone but yourself. You think of no one else."

"But I—"

"But *who*?"

Marianne reddened. The words bit hard. No one had

dared be so blatantly honest in pointing out her faults. She wanted to scream out against this guileless Indian woman, but she knew that Essence was being truthful.

"If you truly loved Mr. Abelard, my child, you would be content to live with him anywhere." Essence's lecture found its target. "His work would become your heartbeat. You would not try to discourage him from fulfilling God's call on his soul to be a missionary.

"If he lives, Miss Marianne, you may marry him, but he will be happy only on the surface, only for you. They are the most miserable of God's servants who are half committed. His heart will rust out inside—"

"I am not asking that he not be a parson. He can preach in town at the cathedral."

"It will never work. A cathedral is not where his spirit longs to be. It is with my people that he yearns to work. We have a beautiful culture, Miss Marianne, and we are unselfish. We want the land and the wild animals to be free for everyone. Your people try to possess land and tell others they cannot cross it to hunt or fish. Even now they are trying to buy up our forest to take it away from us. It is not right. All the earth belongs to God, and it must be shared by anyone who has a need for it. Our people must hear about the Savior who died for them, and who will tell them if we haven't a missionary?"

Marianne sat quietly, convicted by what Essence had said.

"Mr. Abelard fights a grave battle now. It is not only a physical battle but a spiritual one as well. He is torn apart by his loyalties: you and his ministry. He may not recognize this, but I have looked into the conflict of his soul. It revealed itself in his eyes when I spoke of my brother and the Kotopaxi tribe."

When Essence mentioned the Kotopaxis, Perregrine thrashed about on his cot, moaning.

"See? His soul responds to the name. If you cannot accept Mr. Abelard as he is, as a missionary, and share willingly in his calling, please do yourself and him a favor by not marrying him."

"Then who will take care of *me*? He said he would—"

Essence looked at Marianne reproachfully. "You are still so concerned about Marianne only? I have offered my heart and my hands. What more can I do?"

A flame of guilt swept over Marianne, but she stamped it out. Had she let it burn away the dross, she would have been a better person. "I will go back to Philadelphia."

"With strangers?"

"With anyone who is going that direction."

Essence saw that she had failed; Marianne meant to desert the dying man. "Then please make sure that Mr. Abelard's brother in Philadelphia knows of Mr. Abelard's condition."

"I will. And I must take with me the brooch and the rings that Perry collected from my aunt's body. She would wish me to have them. They are in his coat pocket."

"Get them. And should the man survive, what shall I tell him?"

"Tell him that if he wishes to marry me, he will find me in the city. I cannot take the wilderness or his groanings any longer. I shall lose my mind here."

Marianne waited her chance to leave. However, the traders did not come that week or the next. And still Perregrine gasped for one breath after another.

Chapter Fifteen

Robin's Return

"Lewis, I am worried sick about Robin," Marie Abelard pestered. She watched the door for Robin's return, but her watching proved fruitless. Her endless hours of prayer finally turned to tears for the motherless girl she loved. "There's a reason Robin hasn't come back."

"Mother, Robin is accustomed to fending for herself," Lewis replied. "Please don't fret over her."

"I can't help it, Lewis, I can't help it. She had one small job, then we planned to make gingerbread cakes—and she simply disappeared!"

He laughed. "Such a fuss over a parlor maid!"

"But she was my *friend*, Lewis. I am in a new country; I know no one except Robin."

"And Margot Payne," he teased.

"Please, let us forget her."

"I shall introduce you to some of the neighbor ladies."

"You know that I am a plain woman, Lewis. I will not fit with your society friends. With Robin, I didn't have to dress up in airs. She was like the daughter I never had—" The more Marie talked, the more over-wrought she became.

"Mother, Mother!" Lewis took her hand, a soft hand beginning to wrinkle. "If Robin means that much to you, I am sure that we can locate her. Or we could just sit tight, and she will show up to clean next week. She has never missed an appointment to clean my quarters."

"I don't want to wait! She may be ill or injured or in some danger!"

Lewis hooted at the idea. "She's as tough as a wharf rat, that one."

"She mentioned wharf rats," Marie said. "She said she lived on the waterfront in one end of a big ware-house. Will you help me find her, please, Lewis?"

"A warehouse . . . let's see . . ." He drew his brows together like angry caterpillars facing each other for a fight. "There's the Wyck Warehouse, but it's mostly a storage building. I don't think it would be fit for human habitation."

"Wherever she lives is not very commodious," Marie supplied. "When she invited me to stay with her, she—"

"She invited *you* to stay with *her*?"

"Why, yes. I was sitting on your front stoop with no key to get in. She didn't know who I was. When she came to clean your rooms and found me outside, she offered to care for me."

"She thought you were a vagrant?"

"She thought I was a human needing love," volleyed Marie defensively. "I have met a great many people in my life, Lewis, whose smallness of soul troubled me. On the other hand, Robin is the most beautiful girl I have ever known. Anyway, as I was saying, Robin said she had but a paltry place to offer, but I would have to defend myself against the wharf rats."

"I'll go look for her." Lewis started for the door.

"I'll go, too."

Marie huffed to keep up with Lewis's long-strided walk. "Not so fast, Lewis," she panted.

The warehouse, weathered to a sickly gray, squatted low and faced the sea. One end was lifted off the ground on rotting wooden stumps. Wide doors for loading and unloading merchandise commanded an entire side, but on the south, a low door, hardly more than a crawl hole, could be seen. Lewis stopped when he heard low singing. He listened for a while, and when he was satisfied that they had found her, he called her name.

Robin put her head out the small door cautiously, squinting her eyes against the sun's reflection on the water. "Why, Mr. Abelard—" Her mouth flew open in surprise. "How art thou finding where I am sleeping?"

"My mother gave me some helpful hints. She was worried sick when you did not return."

Robin saw Marie, and her eyes danced. "Mrs. Abelard, I am so glad to be knowing that thy son is returning safely. How is thy other son being?"

"He is well, we are sure," Marie answered, immediately turning the conversation back to the problem at hand. "Why did you not return to make the gingerbread, Robin?"

"Oh, I cannot be doing that, Mrs. Abelard. The lady thy son is wedding is telling me I am causing much problems and that I am going away before she is reporting me."

"Who told you that?" Lewis asked.

"Thy mother is knowing her." Robin nodded toward Marie. "The red fingers and lips for painting. The high-on-the-nose girl."

Lewis turned to Marie. "Do you know of whom she is speaking, Mother?"

"Probably Margot Payne."

"Margot Payne told you what, Robin?" probed Lewis.

"She is saying that is not legal if I am staying on the night at the room with Mrs. Abelard. She is saying I must not be going back for saying good-bye. It is the ruling of the house man. I am being afraid. She is troubling for me. I am not wanting to be causing hurt for thee. I am coming here to mine home and I am not knowing what I must do. I am crying because I am so missing my friend, Mrs. Abelard."

"There is no rule against a tenant having any visitor he wishes at any time," Lewis said. "I cannot imagine what Margot was talking about."

"She is giving me the bad look."

"I think she was jealous of Robin, Lewis," Marie said.

Lewis roared. "Jealous of Robin? Hardly! But I shall certainly speak to her and see why she would tell Robin such a thing."

Tears pooled in Robin's eyes. "I am not wanting to be troubles."

"Oh, my dear child!" Marie reached forward to clasp Robin to her bosom. "You are no trouble. I am so sorry for the misunderstanding. You must come back, of course. You can share my room with me. There is a trundle for you under my bed. And we shall make gingerbread cakes for Lewis every day."

"Now that sounds like a delicious idea!" grinned Lewis. "By all means, you must come with us, Robin, if you can inspire such sweets."

"Here, let me help you pack your things," Marie said, squeezing past Robin and into the small entrance.

What Marie saw beyond the low opening made her clasp her hand to her mouth to keep from crying out in protest at the privation about her. The room was an airless cell deprived of the sight and smell of sunlight and salty air. It was a piteous little cube with only a dirt floor, the epitome of poverty and misery. In one corner, a pile of papers and ragged canvas served as a bed. *No wonder the rats came,* thought Marie, *to such an inviting nest.*

"Where are your clothes?" Marie asked.

Robin spread her hands over her skirt, a faded earth brown. "All they are on mine back."

"You have nothing more?"

"None, mem. I am washing at night so they are drying while I am closing mine eyes for sleep. If not dry they are in the next day, I am wearing them so not dry."

"Bring all you have with you, Robin." Marie's face was grim. "I will tell Lewis to inform your landlord that you will no longer be renting this place."

"But mem, thou art not understanding. I must have a home."

"You will have a home with me."

"Oh, no, mem!" She looked down at her worn dress. "I am no fitting for thee and thy son. I will not be going with thee."

"Robin," coaxed Lewis, his voice bargaining, "my mother needs you. She has come to a new and strange country, and she has no one for companionship. I will pay you well to stay with her. My work takes me away for many hours a day, and I will not worry about her health and well-being if you are there. Please oblige me—"

"I will no taking the pay." Determination rode in Robin's dark eyes. "It is thou I must be paying. If thou art needing me, I will be coming." She paused and looked about anxiously as if contemplating a hidden worry.

"Is there a problem, dear?" queried Marie.

"If thou art not liking mine, I have then nowhere to home. This," she swept her hand across her pitiful lodging, "will be gone. Maybe someone else is renting. Then where am I going?"

Her simple appeal touched Lewis. "If it doesn't work out for us or for you, Robin, I will talk to Mr. Wyck and get your room back for you," he said. "Is that fair enough?"

"It is too much fair of thee, Mr. Abelard."

"I am sure that everything will go great between you and my lovely mother."

"And thou wilt be explaining to the painting-face lady that I am staying because thou art telling mine so?"

"I certainly will tell her."

Chapter Sixteen

Messages

Three things happened on the following day. Lewis returned to work. Abe King brought the message from Perregrine. And Margot Payne came to call.

Marie served buttered flapjacks with hot vanilla syrup for breakfast. Robin tried to help while taking care to stay out of Marie's way. "I am soon learning the flappingjacks," she said, "and thou canst be staying in the bedding when I am doing this for thee."

"I didn't bring you here to wait on me, Robin," Marie said. "We will do everything together."

"And if I eat like this every morning," laughed Lewis, "I won't be able to bend over to pick up my carving tools!" He snatched his hat and ran for the door. "It is wonderful to have you with me, mother of mine. Now you two stay out of trouble while I am away today."

"It is good to see thy son happy," Robin commented.

Marie's eyes collected moisture. "Yes. It is as I dreamed it would be and better. I have Lewis and I have you. Now if I can only see my younger son, Perregrine."

"He is alike this one?"

"Oh, no!" chuckled Marie. "He is nothing at all like Lewis. Lewis is the happy-go-lucky one."

"I am not knowing the 'happy-go-lucky' what it is meaning."

"Lewis takes life as it comes, laughing his way through. He seldom worries about tomorrow. Many times, his thoughts are not deep. He grows on top of the ground and enjoys the sunshine. You understand?"

"Yes, very good."

"Perregrine, my son who is five years younger, is quite the opposite. His concerns run deep, down to the taproot of his soul. From the time he was just a wee lad, he was serious about life and living. He is often sad for those who do not have salvation."

"I am doing the same thing for the peoples I am working for. Some are not wanting God. God is too . . . bossing, they are saying. Thou knowest what I am meaning?"

"I think so. They don't want to obey God?"

"That is the right saying! God is saying not to be worldy, not to be loving the money, not being immoral in the mind, to be truthful and no bad wordings always. But they do not be listening to God. They do not be praying. They are only selfish and party, party, partying again. I am wanting to be crying for them. Mine Quaker mema is teaching me wrong and right, the both—and to be choosing the right."

"Perregrine is a missionary."

"I am not understanding the missionary."

"A missionary is someone who goes to people of another race and tells them about Jesus."

"He is going to what peoples, mem?"

"He has a burden for the Indians, the people who were here in America before the first white man came. Many of them are superstitious; they worship gods of all sorts. They know nothing of our Jesus."

"Is it not a working of beauty that thy son is doing?" Robin's face glowed.

"Yes, *I* think so. But sometimes he gets discouraged. When I was still in my homeland, he sent letters telling me how slowly the tribes are responding. Once he was shot at by a chieftain, but his hand saved him."

"He didn't let fear stop him. The enemy, Satan, has tried to destroy him many times."

"I am not yet hearing about thy son's wrecking and hurting that is going by soon. He was not the injured? Mr. Abelard is finding him safe?"

"Lewis didn't find Perregrine, but he found where he had been. He knows that his brother is alive and well."

"How is he knowing that if he is not finding him?"

"He followed the trail that Perregrine took and knew that it was his brother that he followed. You see, Perregrine was in a wood-cutting accident when he was a lad. His arm was severed."

Robin looked confused.

"That means cut off. But Lewis, with his wonderful carving ability, made Perregrine a wooden hand. The wooden hand saved Perregrine's life when the chieftain shot at him. Lewis found part of the wooden hand in a cave. Perregrine had used it for firewood to keep himself warm. Lewis recognized his own carving.

"Then Lewis came to the river and saw where Perregrine had pushed his raft into the water and sailed downstream. Lewis returned so that he would be here when Perregrine comes to Philadelphia."

"I am hoping that thou art hearing from thy son soon. Maybe he is coming today?"

"That would be wonderful!"

It was noon when Abe King came to Elfreth's Court looking for Lewis. "I am his mother," Marie told the man, not without a bit of motherly pride. "He is on his job carving for an important man in the government."

"Mr. Lewis Abelard's brother sends greetings," Abe said.

"My son Perregrine!"

"Yes. He is now with the Ayutook tribe and will be coming to Philadelphia soon. He was well when I left him. He sends a map that will give you his exact location." He handed her a soiled, rumpled piece of paper.

"Thank you, thank you!" Marie clutched the paper, scarcely restraining herself from hugging the bearer of the news. "May I pay you for your trouble?"

"Only with your prayers, madam," he said. "Nothing more." He tipped his hat and was gone.

"You are hearing from your son, Perregrine!" Robin clapped her hands with joy for Marie.

"Yes, and he will be here soon! Then we will make twice as many cakes! For nobody likes sweet gingerbread more than my Perregrine. It is his favorite. He has had none for two years."

That afternoon brought Margot Payne. Her cheeks were redder, her eyes sootier than ever. "I undahstand that Lewis has returned," she said.

"Yes," Marie replied, squaring her shoulders, "my son has returned from his journey and with good news, I am glad to say. His brother, my younger son, Perregrine, was not killed in the massacre—"

"Oh, please, don't talk with such forthrahtness! We want to hear nothing of murdahs and killing. We are in a modahn city."

"We would be foolish to stick our heads in the sand and pretend there is no suffering in the world."

"We should be foolish to pondah it."

"Anyway, Lewis came back to await the arrival of his brother here. Then we shall have a grand reunion, my sons and I! Oh, it was good to see my Lewis again after two long and heart-wrenching years. My joy shall be complete when Perregrine arrives and the four of us are together."

"Foah? Oh, I am so glad that you have included me and that I shall be a part of the gathahing."

Marie had not included Margot Payne in the four; she was speaking of Robin. However, she deemed it wise not to make the correction.

"I have called to invite Lewis to a pahty—" Margot started to say more, but stopped abruptly when she saw Robin dressed in an outfit of soft wool that Marie had made over for her. One could not miss the girl's radiant beauty.

"You have changed your house-cleaning day?" she asked.

Marie didn't give Robin a chance to answer. "Every day is house-cleaning day for us, Miss Payne," she said perkily. "We keep this place spic and span for Lewis, Robin and I do. Just now we are baking cakes against the time when he comes home from work." Marie happened to look past Margot and see Lewis dart around the building out of sight. "But I'm sure he won't be home before you are obliged to leave."

"The maid isn't staying *heah,* is she?"

"Robin's hours are in keeping with her employer's instructions, Miss Payne. He has also ordered her some new clothing and a new winter coat as part of her wages. Her work schedule or her pay is really none of your business, is it?"

"It will certainly be my affaiah when Lewis and I are married!" she retorted.

"Well, until then, it is my affair and Lewis's!" rebuked Marie and impolitely closed the door on a very angry Margot Payne.

Chapter Seventeen

The Trip

In his spare time, Lewis worked on Perregrine's prosthesis. With age his sentimentality thickened like gravy to which flour has been added. He determined to do his best work on this hand. The scare that Perregrine might be dead had worked wonders on Lewis's fickle attitude toward life.

Lewis had made so many "arms" for his brother, he told his mother, he could make them with his eyes closed. With fascination and admiration, Robin watched him work. She ran her hand over the smooth wood, the contour of the fingers. It looked real enough to have life. "This must be the way Adam is looking before God is breathing on him," she said.

Sometimes Lewis took the time to go to Margot Payne's parties, and at other times he didn't. "I don't want that socialite to think she can tell me when to come and when to go," he confessed to his mother.

Apprehensive lest Margot sway her pliable son, Marie reasoned that he should break off all associations with her. He quite frankly admitted that he could not afford such a jeopardy to his business in the city. Her father was a high-ranking official. "I'm keeping my bread buttered, Mother," he said. "But I will not get sand-wiched in."

For a few days, Marie bustled about happily, fed on the ambrosia of hope that Perregrine's homecoming would be any moment. However, when the days stretched into weeks and her son did not show up in Philadelphia, she became first concerned then alarmed.

"He is tied up with preaching to some lost tribe," Lewis predicted. "He will be along by and by."

"No," Marie countered. "Perregrine sent word that he would come to us, and he hasn't. Something is amiss. I must go to him by the map he sent."

"I cannot allow it, Mother," Lewis said. "It is not safe. You do not understand the dangers of this new country. It is nothing at all like our homeland."

"No harm will befall me."

"There's aplenty to harm a lone woman. And one factor is the weather. We are nearing a time of freezing."

"I cannot wait until spring to see Perregrine, Lewis. My heart will not bear the suspense. But I will not travel alone; Robin will go with me. Won't you, Robin?"

Robin looked from Marie to Lewis, torn with the desire to please both of them. "If thou and Mr. Lewis are saying that I go, then I am going with you with much pleasure."

"No." Lewis gave his order and considered it settled.

But it was far from settled. Each new day brought more misery to the worrying mother. She convinced her-self—and then set about to convince Lewis—that Perre-grine was somewhere in dire need of her. It was her first argument in the morning and her last at night.

Finally, she wore Lewis down. "I see that I will have

no peace until you see Perregrine's face," he conceded. "I may as well take a leave from my job and go with you."

"Oh, my Lewis! Will you do this for me?" She gave him a hug. "I am sure he is needing the hand you made for him. He never liked being without it, you remember."

"I can't be away from the city for long, Mother," Lewis warned. "I have several large orders waiting. Government men are not disposed to patience."

"We will not need to make a prolonged visit, Lewis," Marie said. "If Perregrine is in some mighty revival among the natives, we should not distract him with the entertaining of us. As long as I can see his face and know that he is in health, I shall be content with a very short visit. Then he can come to us at his leisure."

"Shall we leave Robin here with the house?"

"Leave Robin here?" Marie's face registered disbelief. "By no means, Lewis. Robin must go along to keep me company on the trip. The rooms will stay clean by themselves. Anyhow, what if that dreadful Payne of a girl should come while we are gone and harass my Robin? I should have a plague of mind from this direction if she is not beside me."

Lewis didn't relish the prospects of the trip. The reminiscence of his recent trek in the woods still clung like a burr to his mind. If the weather turned bad, as it could this time of the year, he might be kept from his business for two or three months. It would not ruin him, but it would definitely set his finances in arrears. Yet he was beginning to agree with his mother. They had heard nothing from Perregrine since the trader's message, and that was a disturbing foreboding. Perregrine's word was his honor. He had said he would come soon, and Perregrine's interpretation of promptness had passed long ago.

"I can hire a carriage, Mother," Lewis mentioned,

"but horseback will be faster. Are you up to it? We have many miles to go."

"I was an ace at horsemanship when I was a lassie," Marie said. "The art will come back to me."

"How about you, Robin?"

"I am riding at mine Quaker mema's home. If thou art getting mine an easy horse and not spooking, I can be riding well, sir."

"Then pack us to go, Mother," acquiesced Lewis.

The first part of the trip went without event. Marie was content to be going toward her last born.

Robin was especially delighted to be out of the city, attuned to nature and the elements. At night, she listened for the trill of the nightingale that sounded like moonlight turned into song. She always awoke early to enjoy the first murmurs of sleepy birds. She didn't know all their voices, but she learned to recognize the wood pigeon's call, his fluted notes clear. The woods seemed full of bird song, full of fragrance, full of life. Its beauty mirrored God's presence.

Hardships did not bother Robin. She handled her horse well and saw to Marie's needs. Lewis allowed that she was an invaluable asset to the trip. He told her so and saw that it pleased her. When she brewed coffee one morning and brought a steaming mug to him, he complimented her. "You are really quite wonderful, Robin."

"That is what I have been trying to tell you all along, Lewis," chimed in his mother. "I would take Robin over Margot Payne any day." Her implication wore no veil.

Robin looked up to find Lewis's eyes upon her, laughing eyes. She lowered her own at once.

On the fourth morning, as they prepared to leave a much-used campsite by a stream, two traders rode up. One of them Marie recognized as Abe King, and she introduced him to Lewis. "This is the man who brought the message from Perregrine," she said.

"And you have not seen my brother since?" Lewis inquired.

"No, we have not been back to the Ayutooks. I am surprised that your brother did not come to Philadelphia, though. That was his immediate plan."

The other trader said his name was Theodore Smyth. *Theodore Smyth.* Where had Marie heard that name before? She sifted through the ashes of her memory, finding it impossible to shake off the feeling that a warning bell had sounded. Smyth . . . Smyth . . . Oh, yes! Robin had mentioned Smyth as the name of her adoptive family and Theodore as one of the older boys. Theodore was her reason for leaving the Smyth family.

She looked about for Robin, but the girl was still at the stream, refreshing herself for the trip. How could she forewarn Robin that Theodore was here, without being obvious?

Marie's mind clawed for answers, but they did not come soon enough. Robin emerged from the break of trees unsuspectingly.

Theodore Smyth's stare bored into the girl, his expression one of victory. "Well, if it isn't mine good sister!" he expostulated. "I have been searching for thee for many years!"

Robin's long-buried fear of Theodore resurrected. Should she flee into the woods, or stay rooted where she stood? Her eyes besought Marie for help. Marie gave a strange and artificial cough, alerting Lewis to some unseen predator.

"You must be mistaken, sir," spoke Lewis quickly, having no knowledge of Robin's previous association with the man. "We are the only family this girl has."

"Yes," vouched Abe King, "the young Miss Abelard

was with her mother at Elfreth's Court when I delivered the message and the map from Mr. Perregrine. I saw her there."

"Well, well," Theodore gave a jittery laugh, "the likeness to mine sister is uncanny! She was a stepsister and no real relative of mine, and it was she that I planned to betroth to mine self to wife. Pardon me, mem, for the mistake."

Still he perused Robin's face, but she kept her eyes averted lest they betray her.

The traders left . . . on their way to the Ayutook tribe.

Chapter Eighteen

Developments

Perregrine still lay in his silent world of sickness, a world from which Marianne blenched. She was like a trapped animal, ready to bolt at the first chance of freedom.

After Essence's frank talk with her, Marianne had made some decisions. She could not marry Perregrine. She would not be happy; he would not be happy. She had been childish and self-centered, and that would change, yes. But she now realized that Perregrine was too good, too noble-hearted for her. He would gladly give up everything for her comfort, and she had not been willing to do the same for him. The love he had for her was one-sided.

With the other chores, she helped Essence, but she could not bring herself to sit beside the sickbed. Her heart was not there. Her spirit would never be with Perregrine, whether he was sick or well. She must go with the traders.

However, when the traders came, they explained that they were on their way farther west for yet more furs.

They promised to stop back through on their way to Philadelphia so that she might travel with them. They would be glad to have such a lovely traveling companion, they remarked. The sly sidewise glances they cast at each other incited Marianne's baser nature.

She was still with the Ayutooks, waiting for the return of the traders, when Lewis, Marie, and Robin arrived to visit Perregrine.

Lewis had imagined his brother stranded with a portly matron rather than a young and ravishing maiden. He listened intently to her story, which she slanted to her own advantage. She identified in Lewis an ally. Here was a kindred spirit, one who would comprehend her present dilemma. They were both as out of place in the wilderness as a fish out of water. If Lewis would only appreciate her refinement in this hideous peasant attire!

Marianne could, indeed, be a charmer, and her good looks only added to the entire composite of her personality. She was gracious and polite to Perregrine's family and to Robin, careful not to mention her engagement to Perregrine. She hoped that Essence would keep quiet about it, too.

She needn't have worried. Essence considered Marianne a poor match for Perregrine and more than hoped that one or the other would change his or her own mind before the final pledge. If Marianne didn't "remember" that she was betrothed to Perregrine, Essence didn't wish to remind her.

Robin, a confederate to back-breaking labor, sized up the situation and concluded that the soft-spoken Essence bore the bulk of the workload. Without a need to be told, she put her shoulder to the tasks at hand and lifted Essence's burden. It was often her job to sit with the sick patient; nursing came naturally to her. Thus, it was late one night around Perregrine's bed that Robin and Essence had time to get better acquainted with each other.

"You have lived in Philadelphia all your life?" Essence asked.

"No. I am maybe coming from over the ocean," answered Robin. "I am not knowing mine background. Only the dreaming over and over is all I am knowing. It is always the same dreaming. In the ship I am going, and then the ship I am going is no more anywhere. I am fighting on the waves until almost I am breathing no more. Then is coming the old, old man with the white beard, and he is taking mine from the water. He is calling mine 'Robin,' a wet soaking bird. From there he is taking mine to a near cabin and giving mine to a nice lady. She is the Quaker believing. She is keeping mine until she is dying. I am running away when she is gone because I am not wanting to be wedding the son. I am too young, and he is not good for mine. Is that making sense to thee?"

"Oh, very much. You were a wise girl. I-I only wish everyone who faced such a decision would be so discerning. But go on with your story, dear."

"Then I am going to be caring for mine self. This job. That job. Other job. It is hard, learning the workings. One lady is saying I must be bowing big and smiling small. But I am forgetting, and I am smiling big and bowing small!"

Essence laughed at Robin's wit.

"I am living in something not so good as your tenting here. Mine is a warehouse. One day Mrs. Abelard is coming over the ocean, and I am finding her sitting on the steps of her son's room. She is saying I must be living with her so that she is no more lonely. I say I cannot. She is saying yes, yes, so many times," she stopped to grin. "I am not saying no, no, fast enough!"

"Mrs. Abelard is a lovely person. And so is her son,"

Essence inclined her head toward Perregrine. "I hope that he may live, but he has the death fever. It will be a miracle if he survives; he has slept too long. I am concerned that he may never awaken."

"Without thee, he would have already died, mem. Thou art like a good angel to him."

"Thank you, Robin. He is a missionary, and our people need missionaries so badly. As I fight the blackness of death, I think of this."

"Thou art always being in thy tribe living in thy tent?" asked Robin.

"I was born and raised here, but I went to stay with my brother for a while after my husband was killed and I lost my children. My husband was shot by a white man. It was a mistake; I hold no bitterness. The white man mistook him for an enemy. Our tribe has been on friendly terms with the white man since he first came. We live in brotherhood and worship the white man's God."

"Thou art speaking the English very good. Much better than mine self. Until Mrs. Abelard, I am not speaking ever much to anyone."

"I had the good fortune to live with a colonial family. My father sent me to their settlement to learn the language so that I might be an interpreter for our tribe. I had a wise father who looked far into the future."

"Thou art having many childrens?"

"Only two."

"Thine is a sad-hearted life."

"Yes, but so is yours."

"Yes," admitted Robin, "until Mrs. Abelard. She is a good angel for mine. She is having no daughter, and I am trying to be making her heart full."

"You are doing a wonderful job."

"If I can be helping her son well again, it is my repaying for her kindness, mem. And so I am praying for him."

While Robin prayed and worried over Perregrine's recovery, Marianne spent her hours roping Lewis's bucking heart. One minute she thought she had him in her grasp, and the next he had slipped the noose. She would like to have won him on her own merits without pulling rank, but she finally became willing to do whatever was necessary to conquer him.

"You are acquainted with my uncle, I believe, Lewis," she said when she needed one more nail to drive into the framework of her scheme.

"Your uncle?"

"Yes, he is a statesman."

"Does he reside in Philadelphia?"

"Yes, he does. His name is Charles English."

"*The* Charles English?" The name-dropping produced the results for which Marianne had hoped.

She lowered her voice to a whisper. "Yes. And since he has no children, he has willed everything to me." She turned her volume back to normal. "Though it isn't public knowledge, he has a bad heart. That is why fate kept me alive."

"This—this is a most unusual circumstance. You are the young lady I wished to meet. . . . That is, I had heard that Mr. English's niece would be arriving. . . ."

Marianne donned her most alluring smile. "He has been most generous with me, my Uncle Charles. He sent me to a prestigious finishing school in London after the tragic death of my parents.

"Do you ever wonder, Lewis, why so many bad things happen to good people? After all I have been through, now I lose my beloved aunt in a senseless massacre. Is it any wonder that I am anxious to leave these wild woods and return to the city? After this tragedy, I must put my life back in perspective. I begged Aunt Eleanor not to make the fateful trip because I didn't wish to accompany her. But she was determined—and just when the mayor's son was ready to court me!"

The last half-truth was the spike that sealed the relationship. Marianne saw that it had worked; she had won. A bid for sympathy and Marianne's coyness blended together to toss Lewis's mind into a state of infatuation. Not once did he suspect that his brother, Perregrine, had an interest in the girl he had rescued.

"Could this be your buttonhook?" Lewis pulled the silver hook from his pocket.

"It is, Lewis! Oh, where did you find it?"

"In a cave."

Her eyes sparkled with a violet fire. "It is a sign! A sign that all will be well for me. I will regain my losses."

Boredom worked in Lewis's desultory nature, and when he announced that he must return to the city for a few days to set his affairs in order, Marianne said that she would go along with him. Marie insisted on staying with Perregrine, and Lewis thought Robin should stay for Marie's sake.

It was the perfect panacea Marianne had hoped for; she couldn't have done better had she planned it all herself.

Essence pulled Lewis aside. "I am not sure that your brother will make it," she said.

"He is much worse? He will not live until I can return?"

"He is neither better nor worse. He may cling to life for a few more days, or the end may come suddenly."

"Please, send for me if he worsens."

"And you will do a favor for a friend? For Essence?"

"Anything in my power, my dear lady."

"You know the government men in Philadelphia?"

"Many of them."

"They are making a bill that is not to the benefit of

the Ayutooks or the Kotopaxis. It concerns the selling of our land. You will not let them take away our tribal lands and send us away?"

"It is a promise, Essence. I will talk to the proper authorities. I will get them to put in a stipulation that excludes your tribes. It is a small repayment for the care you have given my brother."

"Oh, thank you, thank you!"

Before Lewis and Marianne reached Philadelphia, Marianne's skillful angling began to pay off. She had convinced Lewis that he was a perfect candidate for matrimony, the bride being none other than herself. A wedding would be advantageous to both of them; it would advance his business and cure her homelessness.

When the traders returned to the Ayutooks, Marianne was gone. Disappointment rested keenly on their faces. Robin kept her distance from the men, divining that Theodore Smyth would ask if she wished to take Marianne's place. She had no desire to speak with him; he still seemed to question her identity in his mind. She had no doubts that he recognized her, and she was glad when they moved on.

After the departure of Lewis and Marianne, the days fell into a ritual of sameness as Perregrine gained strength in minute increments. Indeed, his progress was so slow as to be almost imperceptible. Marie fretted that he was so changed, so thin. The planes of his face had sharpened. It was clearly the face of a man who had been through the valley of the shadow of death.

Robin waited on him tirelessly. Sometimes she would hold his hand for hours as if to force some of her own health and energy into his inert body. He *must* live!

"You are working too hard," Marie reprimanded.

"Nothing is too hard for God's missionary," Robin said. "Life is not meant to be easy. It is a fighting for life. It is for mine a privilege to be working for such."

At last, Perregrine's eyes fluttered open, and he looked about wildly as if searching for someone. "Marianne . . ." His tongue was thick, making speech difficult. "Marianne . . ."

Robin bent over him. "Can I be helping thee, sir?"

"Marianne . . ." he repeated. "I cannot live without . . ." His voice trailed off and ended with a little cry.

Robin went to Essence. "He is calling for the Marianne. What must I tell to him?"

"Do not tell him that she is gone. Not yet. It might set him back. He is in love with Marianne." Essence kept her explanation simple. "He plans to marry her. When he finds that she has returned to the city, I'm afraid he will miss her dreadfully."

Robin's heart plummeted. Until this moment, she had not reckoned with her own feelings. Now she felt a crushing disappointment that Perregrine loved Marianne then censured herself sharply for her emotions. What right had she, a nobody, to entertain a shred of hope for the attention of a man so holy, so far above herself? The truth hurt, but she was glad that she knew. She had no illusions that she could fill Marianne's place in Perregrine's heart.

Marie was sitting with her son when his mind made the journey back, out of the spectral country in which his unconsciousness had confined him. "Mother?" He blinked his eyes. "Mother!"

"It is all right, my Perregrine. You will be well soon."

"Oh, I am having another vision! I am seeing my mother, and she is across the ocean. Does this mean that after the bitter struggle, I shall die?"

"Perregrine, it is no vision. I came to America on a ship so that I might see my sons again. A Mr. King told me that you were here and gave me the map you sent."

"You have already seen Lewis?"

"Yes, Lewis brought me here. And he made a new arm for you."

"I want to see him . . . to thank him."

"He had to return to Philadelphia to his business; he has many customers waiting. You have been ill for a very long time, my son. But the terrible fever is gone. Every day will be a better day now."

"Where is Marianne?"

"She went back to the city, too."

"I'm glad. She went to ready everything for us. Mother, did Marianne tell you that we plan to be married? She is quite alone in the world, and the Lord has made her my responsibility."

"She didn't tell me, but that is good news, Perregrine! I was afraid that you would be the one of my sons who would never bring me a daughter-in-law. But how strange is life! Lewis tells me that he will never marry, and you tell me that I shall be blessed with a daughter-in-law. And such a beautiful one, Perregrine!"

"She is . . . lovely. I hoped that you would not be unhappy."

"Why should I be unhappy?"

"I will not be able to continue with my work for God."

"But, Perregrine! You must not say that! You will work the better for the Lord with a faithful helpmate. One can put a thousand to flight, but two can conquer ten thousand!"

"Marianne does not wish to be the wife of a missionary. She is not at all suited to the work. She is terrified of the woods, the wild. She loves God but in a different capacity than you or I. I cannot expect her to change. It is I who must make the adjustments."

"Perregrine, the gifts and calling of God are without repentance. It is a promise you made to God—"

"Please do not try to dissuade me, Mother dear. Such a turmoil of soul I have been through heretofore! I pledged myself to care for Marianne, and I cannot go back on my word. She would be heartbroken, and who would care for her needs? The poor child has lost so much in life—all of her blood relatives. I must not let her down. She is such a delicate and lovely flower."

"Neither can you let God down, my son."

"What can I do? Can't you see that God has now called upon me to sustain Marianne? Even now she is in Philadelphia preparing for her wedding—*our* wedding—and I must go to her as soon as I am able to travel."

"We will make it a matter of prayer, Perregrine. God will show you His way. He can change Marianne's heart."

Chapter Nineteen

Margot's Reaction

Margot Payne's indignation became a malignant tumor when she learned that Robin had gone on a journey with Lewis and Marie. Black wrath consumed her.

She concluded that although Robin was not at all in Lewis's social strata, Marie Abelard was pushing for a match between the housekeeper and her son. Marie had dressed the girl in finery, fancied her hair, and bought her some button shoes. As far as Margot was concerned, Marie might as well have attired a skunk in lace. She churned with jealousy.

She watched Lewis's apartment daily for the arrival of the trio. And when she saw Lewis enter his apartment alone, she was more than pleased. She quickly adjusted her thinking, now telling herself that the whole trip was a ruse of Lewis Abelard's to dump his mother and the unwanted maid trying to be a queen.

Margot rushed to Lewis's door with an invitation to the latest ball, a top-drawer banquet that would be populated by "everyone important in Philadelphia." He told her that he would be delighted to attend the party if he could bring along a guest. Otherwise, he said, he wouldn't be there.

Supposing that Lewis meant a male friend, Margot smiled her consent and said that she would inform the host that Lewis would have an out-of-town guest. They would be seated beside her, of course, for an enchanting evening.

On the night of the party, Margot waited for Lewis in the foyer of the mansion. He was late; that was unlike Lewis. The clock had already pounded out seven gongs, and she had told him to be there precisely at six forty-five. He should have dropped whatever he was doing and kept the date. She grew more agitated as the moments ticked away.

Margot had worn her most intoxicating fragrance and a revealing evening gown. These things always allured men, and Lewis was no different from the rest.

The ballroom was alive with shimmering dresses. Silk skirts rustled, immature girls tittered, and men bowed dotingly to all the ladies. A breath of perfume hung in the air. This was the city's elite flaunting their wealth in jewels and velvet. This was Margot's world. This was Lewis's world.

The band struck up a symphony, its soft strains fragmented by the clatter of crystal wineglasses. Where was Lewis Abelard?

Suddenly, she saw him gliding in the door with a . . . with a stunning young woman! She had her hair drawn into a topknot with copper and golden curls at her forehead and at the nape of her graceful neck. The light from the lamps caught in her flaxen tresses, giving them a luxurious blaze. Her long-lashed violet-blue eyes were set widely apart. Was this siren Lewis's escort, or had they simply arrived simultaneously?

Lewis held out his hand to Margot. She took an eager step forward, greeting him with nervous relief. "Margot the lovely!" He bent in the middle and kissed the tips of her fingertips. "I hope that we did not keep you waiting long. Margot, may I present my future bride, Marianne."

In a warm, clear voice, Marianne said, "I am pleased to meet you."

Margot was as nettled as an angry wasp. Envy dug trenches in her aplomb. This gorgeous beauty fell not one whit behind the arbiters of fashion. Lewis was teasing, of course. He was good at that. Could this girl be Lewis's cousin? Niece? Lewis wasn't actually planning matrimony, of this Margot was certain. He had pulled practical jokes on her before, but this was carrying things a bit too far.

Now she would not have Lewis's full attention for the evening's festivities. The girl, whomever she was, had botched everything. And Lewis's impious joke about marriage infuriated Margot.

Catching Marianne talking earnestly to an older gentleman, Margot managed to cloister Lewis beyond the heavy drapes, pushing him onto a small balcony where they could be alone. "Lewis, I am offended at your jesting," she said testily.

"What jesting, Margot?"

"The *wife* joke." There was a glint of madness in her eyes. "That isn't fair when you know how I feel about you and the plans I have for us."

"I am as serious as consumption, Margot. I met Marianne on my most recent trip and fell head over heels in love with her. I know that doesn't sound reasonable, but I have heard that love has neither rhyme nor reason. And I am now convinced that it is so. It happened quickly and caught me by surprise. But we match, Marianne and I. We enjoy the same lifestyle. We share the same values and adhere to like principles. We have the makings of a successful marriage. She has had some misfortunes, and I hope that I shall be able to provide well for her to compensate for her losses. She will be a blessing to me. My mother told me that I would know when I had found the right woman—and I know I have found her.

"We shall be married at Swedes' Church. Marianne is quite fond of that particular sanctuary. She is planning a large church wedding, and I hope that you will be able to attend."

"Where—where did you meet her?"

He laughed. "Of all places, out in the wilderness. She has but recently come to America."

Margot's eyes took on a calculating fire. She would not let Lewis Abelard slip through her fingers so easily. The flame of his infatuation could be extinguished as quickly as it had been ignited. She knew just how to douse it; her ploy was sure to work.

"I will see that youah business is ruined if you marry that strangeah, Lewis. She is an outsidah. And think of it: when youah resouahces are gone, how long will she stay with you?" She enjoyed the taste of her bitter tongue. "You know that my fathah holds a key position with the govahnment. He has been responsible for many of the lucrative assignments you have enjoyed. If you want to keep youah job, you will drop this Marianne girl and come back to me. It is *I* who can be most advantageous to your futuah. I hold youah success or failuah in my own hands." Her eyes became the gray of a frozen lake. "Certainly you are not using youah good sense. A pretty girl with an empty head has swayed you."

Lewis let her rant on, refusing to agree or to contradict. When she had finished her tirade, he backed away. "Pardon me, Margot, but I must get back to Marianne," he said. "She will wonder what has become of me."

140

At the table, an irate Margot was seated beside Marianne. It was the arrangement she had asked the host to accomplish, thinking that she would be flanked by gentlemen who would lavish their attention on her. Instead, Lewis's adoring gaze was upon Marianne the entire evening. There was a worshipful look on his face such as Margot had never been afforded. It galled her.

Marianne placed Margot's jealousy for what it was, and her eyes filled with secret amusement. She dropped her conversation to a low pitch so that maximum attention was immediately secured, keeping those about her mesmerized. Lewis's smile showed that he was proud of her.

When the meal had ended, Margot sought out her father to begin her campaign against Lewis. This inane romance would be nipped in the bud. However, she found her father in conversation with his superior, the Honorable Charles English.

Margot stood to one side and waited, daring not interrupt such an important member of the cabinet. But to her chagrin, Marianne waltzed up and kissed Mr. English on the cheek. For a brief moment, the two stood in mysterious isolation, Mr. English shutting everyone else out.

"My Lewis is ready to go now, Uncle Charles," she said loudly enough for Margot's ears. "He will call on you tomorrow for his appointments. I wanted to say good-bye." She floated away.

Margot stood looking after her, defeat written on her face. To speak to her father would avail nothing. She had made an utter fool of herself. When she had threatened Lewis, he had said nothing, all the while knowing he held the winning cards. He was engaged to the niece of a man of greater authority than her father. And Lewis hadn't bothered to stop her blustering. He had let her stand there and look like a goose! Her face burned with humiliation.

The whole unfortunate evening was too much for Margot Payne's pride. She booked passage the next day for Great Britain. She was a woman who had enough sense to know when she was bested—and she couldn't hold a candle to Marianne English.

Marie sent word that Perregrine was improving and that Lewis need not make the trip back to the wilderness. They would all travel to Philadelphia when Perregrine was able.

Lewis wanted to wait for his mother's return to be married, but Marianne did not wish to delay the wedding. "Who knows how long your mother will be gone, Lewis?" she reasoned. "I am weary of staying with Uncle Charles's frumpy housekeeper."

They planned to be wed at Swedes' Church with winter ivy, music, and flickering tallow tapers—and a dress for Marianne of oyster silk.

Still Lewis knew nothing of Marianne's former engagement to his brother, Perregrine. He would not have stolen Perregrine's sweetheart for the sum of earth's precious stones.

Chapter Twenty

Homecoming

The spring's first shoots of slumbering green were awakening and lifting their heads from earthen pillows by the time Perregrine's health improved enough for him to make the trip to Philadelphia to keep his promise to Marianne.

He had returned from a far place. It seemed that years had passed since he had seen her. His sickness had blotted out the sharp recollection of her face, the sound of her voice. His memory was mercifully selective. Marianne became a sunlit, lingering dream. He only remembered that she was lovely, and he was anxious to see her again and to make her his own.

Essence, who had accepted Perregrine, Marie, and Robin as her own family, sensed the day of abandonment, and her heart wrestled with thoughts of her own future emptiness. Robin felt Essence's heaviness and seesawed between the desire to remain with Essence and the call of duty that demanded she return to the city with Marie. Each in her own way was as lonely as the other.

When Robin expressed her inner tug-of-war to Essence, the selfless lady offered her advice. "You must go back to the city, Robin. You will want things in life that I could not give you."

"I am wanting only someday to be wedding a man I am loving who is loving mine too," Robin said simply. "But it is only dreams, Essence. I am not knowing mine country over the seas. I am not knowing how old I am; only by the inside I am feeling. How can I be marrying when I am not knowing even mine self? So now I am going on working forever."

There was a special spiritual bond between Essence and Robin though their ages differed by more than twenty years. They needed no words to understand one another. Marie declared it was the two of them bound together in attitude and determination that pulled Perregrine through the near fatal fever. "It's in the Bible," Marie said. "Where *two agree,* the results come. I've never seen two more agreed together than the two of you."

Perregrine, too, saw the sadness in Essence's eyes when their departure time neared. "You can go with us, Essence," he said. "I'm sure Marianne will not mind."

Essence was sure Marianne *would* mind. She and Marianne had nothing in common. "No, I must stay, Mr. Abelard," she told him. "I am very lonely, but this is the place God has assigned to me. I am the interpreter for my tribe; I must always show them God. If no missionary comes, I will do my best with my limited knowledge to lead them.

"I cannot read; I have no Bible. And there are many things that I do not comprehend, but He does. Even though you will no longer be a missionary, you must keep my tribe and my brother's tribe, the Kotopaxis, in your prayers."

Perregrine dropped his head. He wished Essence

would not talk like this. Her words sent a pain to the marrow of his bones. He had carried an overwhelming burden for the Kotopaxi tribe, and now that the door had opened, he was not free to walk through it. How could one fathom God's ways?

Then began their journey, a quiet, plodding time. Perregrine was still weak, and Marie cautioned him to go slowly. It was Robin's knack for seeing to the small details of their comfort that took them smoothly through the long, rough miles. She kept the fires fed and cared for the animals. She had a way of being unnoticeable and unabrasive, traits that often caused her ministrations to be taken for granted.

At night, with Perregrine and Marie bedded down, Robin studied the stars spangled across the velvety heavens, giving special attention to the North Star, a guide for wayfarers through the ages. She sensed a distinct need for guidance for her life. What did the future hold for her?

They crossed paths with the traders again. The two had completed a successful season, they said, trading for many fine skins. Theodore Smyth was more relaxed, almost jovial. He made a point to draw Robin into the conversation, asking her name. When she looked beseechingly at Marie, Marie supplied a fictitious substitute. "Rosalyn," she said, and Perregrine decided that his mother was getting forgetful. Or maybe that was the girl's legal name.

Theodore had matured into a square-jawed, broad-shouldered man. When he smiled, Robin noticed that he was quite handsome. But she didn't want to think of him as desirable lest some wall she had built about her heart begin to crumble. She was uneasy until they rode on.

The last silver glow was fading from the sky when Perregrine, Marie, and Robin reached the edge of the city. Like the rest of the country, the town was moving west. Perregrine's weak body and tired mind threatened to betray him. He had forgotten what a maddening bustle went along with a populated area. He didn't remember how sterile the cobbled streets with their brownstone buildings could appear to a man whose heart had a call elsewhere. Two weeks on the trail had exhausted his emotions. His whole being wanted to turn and flee, flee back to the mountains, woods, and serene streams of water. Could he ever forget them and adapt to this sprawling chaos of tangled avenues and seasoned brick?

God help me, prayed Perregrine. *Help me to be content here with Marianne. Let me never expect her to be what she is not. Let me always love and care for her, and give me the strength and decency never to let her know how I loathe the city.*

Fatigue lodged in Perregrine's eyes. Marie saw it and looked beyond it. The exhaustion was more than physical. Something was bothering her son.

Robin noticed Marie's worried frown. "Here thou wilt be having a doctor, Mrs. Abelard. A doctor can be helping to make Mr. Perregrine strong. Thou must not be worrying."

Horses, carriages, and wagons jostled along noisily with frightening speed and too close together. A few pedestrians cast curious looks at the trio.

They made their way hurriedly to Elfreth's Court to Lewis's apartment. "Lewis will be at work," Marie said, "but I have a key to the house in my purse." She unlocked the door and stepped inside.

The sight that met her, however, made her gasp and back up. New hooked rugs lined the polished floor. There was a padded rocker by the bookcase, and through the bedroom door, Marie saw a strange four-poster bed draped over with a grape satin comforter.

"Oh, dear!" she exclaimed. "Someone else has taken Lewis's rooms! He has moved. We shall have to search for him."

At the outcry from Marie, Marianne came from the back of the apartment. "I thought I had burglars," she said. Her bathrobe of woven silk swirled about her legs. "But do come in, Mother Abelard."

"Marianne!" Marie smiled, a smile made of all they'd shared in the wilderness, and reached out to embrace her. "Please tell us where we may find Lewis."

"He is yet at work," Marianne said, beaming. "He is trying to finish a special project for one of the wives of a legislator." She had quite forgotten that Perregrine existed.

"How thoughtful of him to let you have his rooms and move elsewhere!"

Marianne cleared her throat. When Perregrine moved toward her, she avoided his eyes, nor did she speak to him. "Lewis left a key for you to an apartment that became vacant at the corner of the Court," she said. "He said you were to go directly there. You will wish to get settled in and make yourselves comfortable." She was in polite control of the situation. "I'm sure you must be tired, all of you. Lewis stocked your pantry, but I will be glad to prepare a meal for you and bring it—"

"Oh, no, no! We wouldn't wish to bother you, dear. Robin will help me, and we'll—" Marie began, but Perregrine interrupted.

"Marianne, my dear, we will meet to discuss our future without delay," he said, trying to override Marianne's formality. He moved past his mother toward her, intending to clasp her hand in his own. But Marianne retreated a few steps, and the smile froze on her face.

"Please, no, sir. Lewis will be in shortly and will explain everything. Your apartment is one-seven. Good day." She dropped a key into Marie's hand and fled to the adjoining room. The door's lock clicked behind her.

"Now isn't that peculiar?" murmured Marie, something dawning just beyond her grasp but trying to spread its light to her befuddled mind. "I suppose, Perregrine, that Lewis wanted you and Marianne to live near the rest of us; therefore, he secured the empty rooms for himself. But I wonder, why didn't he keep his own place and lease the vacant apartment for you and Marianne? I must say, it is a great mystery."

"Lewis has never made much sense, Mother," chuckled Perregrine, but even the chuckle came out in nervous strips. "I'm sure he has reasons that are clear only to himself. I find that sometimes the ways of my elder brother are more intelligent than my own. Shall we go to Lewis's rooms now? I will see Marianne when she is properly attired. We quite embarrassed her, I'm sure."

At apartment seventeen, Marie felt quite at home. Lewis's old furnishings sat about in much the same manner as they had occupied the former rooms. His armoire was there, but his clothing was nowhere to be found. "Obviously, he has just made the switch and hasn't moved his personal belongings," Marie mused.

"He probably plans to do that tonight," Perregrine ventured. "We should have a quick feast so that I may help him."

"I must say," Marie proposed, "that Marianne has changed. I am still grieving that you would give up God's work for any woman, Perregrine, but after seeing her, I feel better. She gave us a proper welcome and seems very efficient. I was afraid she would not make you a good wife. You certainly didn't seem to match. But like as not she'll take to domestic life like wildfire taming itself to a hearth."

Perregrine felt gratified by his mother's small concession in regard to his future bride. He had thought she was disappointed. He didn't want to be in the bad graces of both her *and* God. If she approved, perhaps God would too.

Still, his feelings were raw and turbulent. Did he really love Marianne? At least, he had imagined that he did. That was before his illness, before her return to Philadelphia. Now he found he didn't like the way her eyes purposely overlooked him this evening. Something was wrong, and he couldn't put his finger on it. In the wilderness, she had wanted to cling to him; here she pulled away. Did she not need him now?

"You will share a room with Lewis, Perregrine," instructed Marie, glad to have something to challenge her mind, "and Robin and I will room together. You and Lewis had best take the front bedroom so that Lewis may come and go about his job more readily. When you and Marianne are married—which I am sure will be soon—Lewis will have the room to himself."

Robin busied herself in the kitchen, feeling herself an outsider. She would move back to the shed by the wharf, she promised herself, as soon as Marie's family was settled.

They waited for Lewis, but he did not come. A strange silence fell upon all of them. Perregrine excused himself to his room as soon as possible.

While Marie snored softly beside her, Robin tossed and tumbled. Her dreams shifted from the shipwreck to Theodore Smyth and then to her friend Essence. Perregrine Abelard did not figure in the dream at all.

Chapter Twenty-One

Shock

T he next day, Perregrine walked to the ocean front, troubled by an uncertainty that nagged at his soul. It was a curious walk. He wanted to think quietly about Marianne, about what he would say to her. He didn't want to disappoint her; there must be some romance in his words.

Instead, a legion of impressions came rushing into his head, each one vivid, each one struggling against the other for a dominant place. He saw Lithia and her son. He was sitting in her pueblo, telling them about God. He saw the chieftain of the Kotopaxi tribe in full regalia. He saw Essence. When he tried to focus his thoughts on Marianne, the Indians kept getting in the way. He shook his head savagely to be rid of them. He tried to pray, but his prayers were arid.

"Marianne," he whispered. "I am coming, Marianne." When he called her name, he knew the peace of a man who faces reality and knows when he accepts what he cannot change.

Lewis and Marianne came to call while Perregrine was gone. Marianne wore a taffeta dress so blue that in the shadows it looked black. It had a detachable collar and cuffs made of lace. She gripped Lewis's arm.

Robin had never seen anyone so beautiful or a garment so elegant. The city had transformed Marianne.

"I hope that you are comfortable, Mother," Lewis said, giving a bashful laugh that was out of character for him.

"Very comfortable, Lewis," Marie rejoined. "We're still getting situated. I hope that you don't mind us moving in on you. We put you and Perregrine in the front bedroom—"

The sheepish look on Lewis's face made Marie fold her sentence in the middle. "Is that not agreeable with you, Lewis?"

He made a whirring sound in his throat. "Uh, I have something to confess, Mother."

Her motherly intuition lagged. "Confess? What is it, Lewis?"

"Your wish has come true. I have taken a wife."

"Who?" Marie was truly confused. "Not Margot Payne?"

"I married Marianne. Congratulations are in order."

"But Lewis—"

Marianne paled. Knowing an exposé was coming, she tried to intercept it. "I think, Lewis, that your mother supposed that I might marry your brother, Perregrine, simply because he rescued me from the coach wreck."

"But Perregrine said—" Marie began.

"Perregrine was burdened with me for quite long enough, Mrs. Abelard. His care for me was nothing less than heroic, but I am sure he will be relieved that Lewis offered to take me off his hands so that he can get back to his missionary work."

"Where is Perregrine?" This came from Lewis. "Is he well?"

"He is gaining strength. He went for a walk. The salt air will be good for his lungs."

"I shall find him and tell him that he has a sister-in-law."

Marianne tugged at his sleeve. "Please, Lewis. Let your mother break the good news to him. We have an appointment, remember?" Apparently, Lewis did not remember, but he let Marianne hurry him away.

"Well, what do you think about that, Robin?" asked Marie when Lewis and Marianne were gone.

"I am hurting for thy son who is first loving her," Robin said, her voice as soft as a spring rain. "It is hard to help a hurting when thou art not knowing how, isn't it, mem?"

"Yes, it is. It will be a shock to Perregrine. He came back to Philadelphia with full intentions of marrying Marianne. Yet I can't help but be relieved. I prayed that God's will would be wrought, and I could not but worry that Perregrine would have been unhappy on the inside had he turned his back on his calling. Since childhood, he has been disposed to moods of prayer and meditation. Marianne would not have understood those spiritual seasons; Marianne is too shallow."

"Is she the right one for thy Lewis?"

"I much prefer her to the Payne girl."

"Oh, yes, mem. Anything but those redding of blood lips!"

Marie paced the floor and prayed until Perregrine came back. She dreaded imparting the news of Lewis's marriage to him. She had tried to protect her youngest against life's injustices, but still they would come. How bruised he would be by the turn of events she could only attempt to guess. But it would be a blow.

Perregrine had hardly gotten past the threshold when he announced, "It is time that I go to Marianne and plan for the wedding. It will be soon. After my morning prayer, I am ready."

"Perregrine . . ." The pity in Marie's voice when she spoke his name made him whirl about.

"Don't try to talk me out of it now, Mother. The decision is made. I have walked all morning with Marianne's shadow at my side."

"You cannot marry Marianne."

"I will marry her for better or for worse." He pulled out the last outrageous, unpardonable stop. "Marianne needs me worse than God does."

Marie's voice softened even more. "She is already married, Perregrine."

For long, cold seconds, he doubted his hearing, and then he sat down abruptly as if the wind had been knocked from him. "What do you mean?"

"Marianne married your brother, Lewis."

"*Lewis?*" There was a waxen cast to Perregrine's skin, drained of his life's blood.

"They came to tell us this morning while you were gone."

"I don't understand!" He raked the back of his hand across his brow. "Lewis knew that Marianne belonged to me. Why would he—?"

"I don't believe that he did, Perregrine. I don't believe Marianne ever told Lewis that there was anything between you and her. I don't think he knows even now."

"Then he shall never know. You must promise, Mother, that you will never bring the subject up again." He lowered his head. "The fault is mine. I listened to a sweet voice who sang a false song. I wish Lewis happiness and good fortune."

Robin's heart reached to the jilted man. For a

moment, his feelings of rejection and loneliness became hers. He had come to Philadelphia with grand plans, and now those plans lay in shambles.

Marie couldn't bear her son's awed and dreadful silence. "We prayed, son. . . ." She saw a tear drop to the floor. "Do you feel like talking, Perregrine? What will you do now?"

He shook his head wearily. "I don't know, but I will not sit here and be beholden to my brother and his charity. Nor will I daily look into the face of the woman who spurned my offer."

By afternoon, Perregrine's restlessness had reached a fevered pitch. He had eaten nothing at all. "I am going back," he announced.

"Back?"

"Back to the wilderness, to a solitary place. To think. To pray. To start over."

"Won't you rest for a few days?" his mother asked.

"No. I wouldn't rest here."

"You will return to the Ayutooks?"

"I will go to the Kotopaxis. That is where my heart is. It seems I have had to go around the world and back again to get there, but get there I will."

"Oh, Perregrine! Isn't that the tribe at whose hands you almost lost your life?"

"Yes, but things have changed, and now they call for me. I have seen them in my dreams. I shall bury myself so deeply in my work—in God's work—that I will soon forget."

"All things work together for good to those who love our Lord," Marie quoted. "You shall see, my son. You have finished a painful chapter of your life, but the story is not completed."

"I should hope not. I would hate for my book to end on such a dreary page."

"We shall hear from you?"

"I shall send word by our friends, the traders, of my location and my welfare when they are coming this way." His mind was already on his journey, conscious of an undergirding of strength he had begun to doubt was still there.

Marie followed him about, savoring the last few minutes with her son. Robin stayed in the background, uncertain of what to do or say.

"I am glad that you came to America, Mother," Perregrine told Marie. "And thank you for coming to me when I was so ill. If ever you need me, send word by Theodore Smyth."

He had his hand on the handle of the door. "And thank you, too, Miss Robin, or is it Rosalyn?" He gave her one quick, detached glance, but his gaze seemed to go through her or past her.

"I am saying the prayers for thee every day, Mr. Perregrine," Robin said demurely. "It is the most important thing in the world to be a missionary, sir. And thou wilt please give mine love to Essence when thou art seeing her again."

"I will." Perregrine hurried away.

Marie looked after him until he was out of sight. She shook her head. *A tree bent by harsh winds often bears the richer fruit.*

Chapter Twenty-Two

The Tribe

A king's welcome awaited Perregrine when he arrived at the Kotopaxi tribe. Young Victor, called Broken Bow until a year ago, met him with glad recognition. At thirteen, the boy was tall and sinewy, as tall as Perregrine. He took the missionary first to his mother, Lithia, and Lithia took him to the chieftain.

Communication was a problem. The chieftain spoke no English, and Perregrine's command of the Kotopaxi language was limited to a sketchy vocabulary. The chieftain, soul hungry and open to the gospel, decided to send for his sister, Essence, to act as an interpreter.

Essence's delight and surprise at seeing Perregrine were equally proportioned. She had understood that he would marry Marianne and give up his missionary work. When she learned that there had been no marriage, her eyes shown as if they had absorbed the morning sunlight. "Happy you would have been for a year, maybe two," she told Perregrine. "Then your heart would have returned to us while your body stayed in the city. It is not good that a heart and body be divided. It troubles the mind."

At that moment, Perregrine felt that Essence had painted his portrait. His heart was still in Philadelphia with Marianne, but his body was here. But he said nothing. He was glad he had not stayed in the city long enough to see Marianne again. The pain would have consumed him. As he swam back in the brook of his memories, he saw her now, holding his hands as he lay in a fog of fever. Would the hurt ever go away?

The chieftain asked many questions about God. He wanted to learn everything at once, gobbling up knowledge like a starved man. Perregrine had never witnessed such ready soil for planting the seeds of God's Word. For several days, he made the teaching his sole focus.

"I believe," the chieftain said. "I believe your words about God coming to the earth as a man to die for my sins. I have believed for a year. I have put away all the sins that I know. I have been waiting for you to come to my tribe and baptize me and Lithia and my son, Victor, in the name of Jesus like the Christ's men did it. We are waiting for God's Spirit to fill us and cause us to speak with His new language, and I know that He will."

For one brief span of time, a fulfillment such as Perregrine had never experienced swept away his pain. Nothing mattered but this: leading lost souls to the Master.

Then the carnal yearnings welled up again. If only he could have had this and her, too. His thoughts had crept away, and he almost didn't catch what Essence was saying. "My brother needs advice," she repeated.

"I hope that I can help," Perregrine said.

"Some of the tribal members want to hold to the old traditions," she translated for the chief. "When Lithia told me of the true God to whom you had introduced her, I ordered the totem poles destroyed. The medicine man died, and I refused to appoint another. The scalpings came to an end at my command. I have pronounced a punishment for anyone who breaks my laws. They will be put out of the tribe.

"Yet there is dissension within my tribe. I know that some of the tribal members have hidden idols, gods of wood and stone. There is one young man named Slate who keeps the braves stirred up. He is young but powerful. He would like to show his physical prowess by plundering and killing the white man. He does not like the law of neighbor loving neighbor or returning good for evil. He thrives on bloodshed. His mother, Keeta, is the scandal monger among the squaws. Both of them try to make trouble for my wife and my adopted son. It is not good.

"What can I do to make this young man—and all the tribe—serve God? I am the chief, and they are afraid to disobey openly, yet not all in my tribe are true hearted. It is a great problem. I need your advice, please."

"No one can force another to serve God," Perregrine explained. "Christianity is a matter of the heart, and love comes from the Spirit. A man-made law cannot bring about a change in anyone. That is why Jesus came. The old law of Moses did not grant power over sin. It could not accomplish the changes needed inside us. Jesus came to make a new law, a law written in the heart. Only Jesus can change a person *inside*."

"Then what can I do?"

"We must pray to God and ask that He do whatever is necessary to turn Slate and those he influences around."

"He has much anger and rebellion."

"God has much grace and forgiveness."

"Will you talk to the young man?"

"If I am to talk to the young man, God will have to open two doors: the door of opportunity for me and the door to the young man's heart."

The chieftain nodded.

Essence stayed in the small pueblo that had once housed Lithia and her son, but the chieftain insisted that Perregrine stay with him in his large pueblo. There were many rooms: a room for each bed, a room for the table, a room for the oven. Bolsters stuffed with feathers lined the chairs, and even the floors were covered in sheepskin. Perregrine's room was complete with gourd bowls, water pitchers, and guest moccasins.

With furnishings so accommodating, maybe Marianne would have—

He chopped the thought short and plunged into the life of the wilderness with a vigorous desperation.

Chapter Twenty-Three

The Meeting

Perregrine awoke with a start. He had seen Marianne's face in his dreams. She was running away from him. Just when he thought he could reach out and embrace her, she would increase her speed or sidestep, and his hands grabbed at empty air. Fragments of the dream that floated up like driftwood on the shoals of his mind so disturbed him that he dressed hastily and went for a walk in the woods as was his habit when he was especially agitated.

The first pale fingers of sunshine were feeling their way among the trees. So fast was his pace that he almost plunged headlong into Slate. In the thick shadows, the large boy-man was impassive as if he were not a human but a marble statue. There was a curious sense of unreality about him. One was as surprised as the other, and for a dreadful moment, neither moved.

Perregrine recognized the man he faced. This was the Indian who had attacked the stagecoach! In a terrible flashback, Perregrine saw it all: the arrow protruding from the body of Mr. Flanders, the horses bolting, the driver trampled, and the face of the Indian. No one had to tell Perregrine that this was Slate, the chieftain's troublemaker. He knew.

Perregrine's weight failed to equal half of the massive man before him, yet it was Slate who quailed. He was caught. If Perregrine reported his ambush to the chieftain, Slate would be excluded from the tribe, turned out into the wilds with no home and no future. Then what would become of Keeta, his mother? They would lose everything they possessed, be driven into exile, and wander aimlessly. He hadn't a strong enough following to overthrow the tribe nor a number of antagonists sufficient to start a new tribe.

Before Perregrine, with suffocating proximity, stood the culprit who was inadvertently responsible for his present heartache. Had Slate not occasioned Eleanor English's death, then Perregrine would not have been left with Marianne. He would not have made the plans to marry her, the plans that went awry. She would not have had the chance to jilt him for Lewis. Perregrine would not have dreamed of her last night. . . .

Perregrine wrestled with many human emotions, not of the least of which was anger. A quiet, cold rage rose in him. He clenched his fist and swallowed hard. He would relish the chance to have Slate banished from the tribe. It would serve him right! No revenge could be sweeter.

Slate looked at Perregrine as if he could read the missionary's thoughts. He united his hands in front of him in a tight, beseeching grasp that combined apology and contrition. He motioned for Perregrine to follow him.

Perregrine stood rooted. He would not deliberately walk into a trap set by Slate. This rascal had already caused him enough grief.

The overgrown boy motioned again, but Perregrine

ignored him. There was a plea in the boy's eyes. Still Perregrine did not move.

Then Slate made hand signs for Perregrine to stay where he was. He would return, he signaled. He turned and slipped away.

Slate had scarcely slid out of sight when Perregrine's conscience smote him. He had wanted to hurt Slate and in the hurting to ease his own pain. Somewhere he had lost his perspective. He had come to this tribe to reach its lost. Now, instead of wanting salvation for his enemy, he sought to avenge himself. How far he had strayed from the nature of Christ into his own carnal nature! He had not been praying as he should. He had been sidetracked by his fleshly desires.

So far had he wandered from God's character and purpose for his life that he was not worthy to be called a messenger of the Lord. How could he guide the mighty Kotopaxi chieftain to God when his own heart was not right? What right had he to baptize anyone? If your enemy asks you to go a mile with him, then go two, the Master said. Yet Perregrine would not go one step with Slate.

Perregrine Abelard bowed his head in shame. In the moss below a tree, he made an altar for himself and repented in bitter tears. Slate, the murderer, needed to be saved as surely as the thief on the cross needed a cure for his sins. The chastened missionary's prayers turned to supplication, and his supplication turned to travail.

When Slate returned, Perregrine was still lost in intercession with tears dripping from his chin. Slate set the trunk he was bearing on the ground and waited respectfully while Perregrine finished his visit with God. He seemed to know that his own future depended upon the outcome of this private war.

When Perregrine opened his eyes, he saw Slate with

his hand on Marianne's traveling trunk. The boy made motions to show Perregrine that he had found the box floating down the river. Perregrine suspected that Slate knew the trunk belonged to a passenger of the stage-coach he had attacked. He may have seen it in the boot of the vehicle. Unless Slate had removed it, Eleanor's purse with the money would still be inside the trunk.

Slate pushed the portmanteau toward Perregrine with his foot. *He wants me to open it,* surmised Perregrine. Could he bear to see *her* clothing, to relive the past? He felt that he was trying to remove bandages from a festering wound. The nearer he got to the wound itself, the greater the pain.

He opened the trunk slowly and found everything as it had been, untouched. There were the petticoats and the stockings and the waists. He didn't want to look at them, to see them, to touch them. There were too many memories, memories that were now a part of the wardrobe of his misery.

The purse was there and the money with which Marianne had planned to purchase her wedding dress. It would be up to him to return it all to his sister-in-law. *His brother's wife. Marianne.*

Slate stood watching him. Perregrine's calling supported him like a separate organ of command having no contact with his mind or emotions. Something in him screamed against the recollections, but the calling let no sound emerge. A thought formed halfway: *If I had not fallen ill and Lewis had not come . . .* The calling suppressed the rest of it.

Perregrine nodded thanks to Slate and managed a small smile. Then he crooked his finger in a gesture for Slate to follow him. The giant of a boy followed as meekly as a child.

It was obvious that Slate was frightened. Perregrine

directed him to Essence. With no one but Essence understanding the two-way conversation, Perregrine told Slate that he would not report his crime to the chieftain if he was willing to repent. Essence came back with the answer from Slate that he was ready to repent if Perregrine would please tell him how.

Slate repented that day, and Perregrine's grief over Marianne was swallowed in joy. When he saw Slate hold out his hamlike hand to Victor in a pledge of peace and friendship, he allowed his heart might burst.

Slate's mother was the next convert, then one by one the tribe's idol worshipers joined those who believed in Christ. There were no dissenters.

"Marie and Robin will be so happy!" rejoiced Essence. "I wish they were here."

"When the traders come again, I will send word to my mother," Perregrine told her. "And if the traders are able to transport it, we will send the trunk to Marianne."

"I am glad to see that you are back to God with your heart," Essence affirmed. "You have been gone from Him since your sickness."

"It was hard, Essence," Perregrine confessed to the woman who made confession easy, "to give up Marianne."

"I suppose I have never understood why it was so hard for you, Brother Perregrine," said. "Your goals and the girl's goals were far apart."

"But when one finds a woman so attentive, one easily becomes attached," responded Perregrine. "For all those weeks, Marianne sat beside me, never leaving me while I wrestled with the death angel. Many times I heard her praying that I would survive. She held my hand in her own. She was so faithful to me until—" He stopped when Essence gave him a puzzled look.

"But Brother Perregrine, Marianne did not attend

you at all," Essence said. "She did not sit with you a single night."

"It was *you?*" Perregrine's eyes widened.

"No. It was Robin. Robin's prayers plucked you from the jaws of death. And not only her prayers but also her loving heart sustained you. She fed you and bathed your face and held your hand."

"Robin? Who is Robin?"

"The girl who came with your mother."

"Who is she? I thought she was a housekeeper Lewis hired to stay with my mother."

"I don't know who she is—and she does not know who she is—but I would not be a bit surprised to learn that she is an angel. She has a heart of solid gold."

"You know *nothing* about her?"

"She was rescued from the sea, a shipwreck victim, and vaguely remembers clinging to a piece of broken board. She was taken in by a Quaker woman, and she has a sweet Quaker accent when she speaks. But her foster father was not a Quaker. He must have been rather rowdy, and his sons followed his example. When the woman died, Robin deemed it unwise to live with the horde of boisterous men, she being the only girl. She went out in the world to manage for herself at a young age. I do not know the name of the family who gave her a home, but she is grateful for your mother's friendship now."

"I—I'm afraid I was so obsessed with plans for Marianne that I took little notice of anyone else."

"It is a pity."

"And . . . and she is the one who held my . . . my good hand instead of Marianne?"

"Yes. God is my witness."

Chapter Twenty-Four

Marie's Book

Marie's family Bible fascinated Robin, it intrigued her. Mrs. Smyth, her Quaker mother, had possessed one, but the children were strictly forbidden to touch it. Only Mrs. Smyth could read it—and that in her husband's absence. She seldom read it aloud; when she did, the words staggered out haltingly. Robin conjectured that reading was difficult for her.

However, in spite of Mrs. Smyth's own limited education, she was able to teach Robin to read and write. Robin soon surpassed her in ability and comprehension. Unfortunately, God's Word was not a book she was permitted to read. Now Marie gave Robin full access to the Bible. Robin treasured every verse, every line.

She noticed that Marie had written Lewis and Marianne's names in the scrolled section entitled "Marriages." It was located in the book's center. She felt a pang of regret that Marie would never be able to pen Perregrine's name there. He was such a nice man.

Robin had made her own peace with God while

kneeling on the floor of the old warehouse. She had walked with God every day since, but her soul had longed for His Word. She couldn't go to church. She felt that her clothes were unfit for the city church's attendance; besides, she often sat with babies or the ill on Sundays.

Robin found Marie's Bible to be a wondrous book. She spent every spare moment with it. Marie told her it was better to read in the early morning hours while her mind was fresh and rested. She tried to do that; it made the whole day go better.

Marianne came to visit one morning as Robin pored over the Scriptures. "What are you reading, Robin?" she asked.

"I am reading Mrs. Abelard's Bible," Robin said, her eyes incandescent.

"Do you like to read?" Marianne further inquired.

"Oh, yes!"

"I am surprised that you are . . . educated enough." Marianne meant no deprecation, and when she considered what she had said, her face reddened.

"My Quaker mema is teaching me long ago."

"I could bring you a more interesting book," Marianne said. "I am not an avid reader. To be truthful, reading rather bores me. Lewis bought me a book. It is about a girl who fell in love with a Greek soldier, but he had a wife back home—"

Robin's hands flew to her face, and she made a sound of protest. "Oh, I'm not liking to read bad things! I haven't the much time to read, Marianne. I am spending the little time on the good. I am loving the Bible. I am not always understanding it, but I am finding it the most interesting."

"But it seems so dull and . . . and . . ." she sought for a word, "complicated."

"Are thou ever reading it, the Bible?"

"No, but the parson puts me to sleep."

"It is sometimes simple and beautiful. It is sometimes hard to know. But it is God's wording to my heart."

"I suppose that one like you who has never known excitement would find any diversion a pleasure."

"I am not trading if I could. I am happy inside, and the outside is not mattering. The Bible is telling me about a home in heaven. It is much better than all the exciting in the world."

Marianne laughed, her sudden, brittle laugh. "Forethought and afterthought are wasted thoughts," she said. "Yesterday is history and tomorrow is a mystery. I think only of today."

"It is not good to be thinking only of today. Today is passing away. Life is much short. Afterlife is much long. Forever. Here. Let me be reading it to thee: *It is appointed unto men once to die, but after this the judgment.*"

Marianne squirmed, wanting to walk out but not wishing to be impolite.

"And here is one more: *Behold, now is the accepted time; behold now is the day of salvation.*"

"I will have plenty of time to think on somber things when I am old." Marianne's face clouded. "I am young—"

"But thou could be dying in an accident. God is good to keep thee alive yet to be finding His way."

Her brush with death was something Marianne wished to forget but couldn't. She knew Robin spoke the truth. Her life had been mercifully spared.

"Please be thinking on it, Marianne." Robin's voice held a plaintive appeal.

Marianne moved toward the door, hoping to escape. "I will, Robin. I promise." Her exit was a near run.

Marie found Robin puzzling over a verse of Scripture in Psalms. "Problems, Robin?" she asked.

"I am not knowing the meaning of this reading, Mrs. Abelard. *The steps of a good man are ordered by the Lord.*"

That means if we live right, Robin, God will work out our problems and lead us where we should go in life."

"But it is saying 'man,' mem. Is it meaning a woman, too?"

"Yes, Robin. The steps of a good woman are ordered of the Lord as well."

"*Mine* steppings are ordered of God?"

"Absolutely."

"Oh, Mrs. Abelard! It is too much wonderful!"

Chapter Twenty-Five

Theodore

Perregrine had been with the Kotopaxi tribe for three months. The Kotopaxi chieftain urged him to remain with the tribe and be their teacher. "We have much to learn," he said. "We will build you a pueblo much better than my own. God's chief deserves more than an earthly chief." They spun a cocoon of loving kindness about him.

This, then, was why God brought him across the ocean. This was his calling; these were his people. He had found God's will for his life. It was a comforting revelation.

Since his conversation with Essence, Perregrine could not cast the thoughts of Robin aside. He had given her so little notice that the pictures of her he tried to develop in the darkroom of his mind were blurred.

He wanted to talk about her so often that Essence laughed. "You are a bitten man, Brother Abelard, and you don't even know it. Why don't you marry Robin and bring her here? She would make a perfect missionary's wife. She loves God, and she works well with our people."

"Truly, I would like for her to come here, Essence. But she may not wish to marry me. She may not love me. How could she love me when I gave so little notice to her kindness? Oh, Essence, she must think me most ungrateful!" He stopped and looked at Essence aghast. "My sin of forgetfulness has come to torment me. I remember now that she told me when I left Philadelphia to give you her love. She must be quite fond of you—"

"Yes, she and I were the best of friends. We understood each other. She lost her parents, and I lost my husband and children. I have not felt such a bonding to anyone since my own loved ones were taken."

"Would you—could you—invite her here for a visit—and—and see if she could care for me?"

"I cannot write. I don't know how. You must write the letter, our Reverend Abelard, and send it. I will pray that Robin will come."

"If I tell my mother the reason we wish Robin to come, she will send her. My mother wants me to take a wife so she will have another name to write in the middle of the family Bible."

"That's a good reason. I will go back to my tribe and wait for Robin's arrival. When she comes, I will send for you."

Trader Theodore Smyth said he would be glad to deliver Perregrine's letter to Marie Abelard and the trunk to Marianne. Theodore had his own reasons for wanting to make the contact, but the reason for his eagerness to be the mailman escaped Perregrine. He placed the parcel into Theodore's hands with utmost trust.

Theodore's character was colored with a shade of dishonesty, and on the way to Philadelphia, he opened the letter to see if it contained money. (He didn't think to check under the clothing in the luggage for Mrs. English's handbag that held plenty.) Robin's name in the letter commanded Theodore's attention, and he helped himself to reading the entire dispatch.

He licked his lips. Ah, then it *was* Robin. . . . He had thought so all along. There couldn't be a mistaking of those eyes. The tongue might deceive, but the eyes never. And this missionary had an interest in her, did he? Well, he wouldn't get her! Theodore Smyth had claimed her for himself when she was still a child in pigtails. Marie Abelard would never get the letter that divulged her son's intentions. And when Perregrine reached Philadelphia—if he decided to check on the lack of response to his mail—Robin would be married. Married to Theodore Smyth.

Robin needn't know that Theodore had taken a wife and tired of her five years ago. Or that he left the weeping woman to care for his child. That was ancient history. He'd learned a lot about the wooing of women since then: hide your bad traits and show only your good side. It worked every time. He would win Robin yet. He was ready for a new game, a different toy. Should he use the power of threats or the beguilement of promises?

Theodore showed up at Marie's door with a brown suit tailored to fit his broad shoulders, his black boots gleaming, and his coal black hair lying close to a narrow skull tamed with axle grease. "Mr. Perregrine Abelard, thy son, sends greetings," he said, bowing gallantly.

"You bring news of my son!" rejoiced Marie. "Please do come in."

"Yes. He says to tell thee that his work is doing well, and he is in excellent form. The entire tribe got religion."

"Oh! It is an answer to our prayers!"

"Let's see. There was something else." He pretended to ponder.

"Do try to remember."

Theodore cast his eyes about for Robin while he feigned forgetfulness. "It was something about the girl who stays with thee."

"Rob . . . Rosalyn?"

"He calls her Robin."

The color drained from Marie's face. Here was a gap in the fence she had failed to repair. She didn't inform Perregrine that Robin's identity must be protected, that Theodore was a foster brother who had designs on her. "W-what did he say about Robin?"

"He said to tell thee that if thou hast entertained any ideas of him marrying Robin, thou canst put the thoughts aside. He said he could never care for her."

Marie sighed. "Perregrine will never marry. He has been bitterly wounded by a woman. A burnt child is afraid of the fire. The damage is irreparable."

"But I must speak with Robin for mine self, Mrs. Abelard. I now know that she is the girl who lived with mine family in mine boyhood home. I was young and foolish then, and I frightened her. I have changed since; I must apologize to her. As a Christian, Robin will certainly be forgiving. May I see her, please?"

Theodore's appeal, with false sincerity, got the results he wished. Marie called to Robin.

"Robin, Mr. Smyth has some apologies to make," she said. "He is quite humble and sincere. Please hear him out." So saying, Marie left the room. Theodore would want to make amends privately.

Robin sat down in a chair opposite Theodore and twisted her hands together to stop their shaking. Theodore favored her with his most deceptive smile, bringing out his handsome boyishness. "Please, Robin, blot the past from thy mind. Time mends foolishness. A transformed Theo sits before thee today. To think of mine own past brings me much shame."

Robin's hands stopped twitching, but something about Theodore's shifting eyes still bothered her.

"I was brought up by a good mother," Theodore continued. This was safe ground; Robin had loved her adoptive mother. "But I strayed from her standards of behavior and followed in the footsteps of mine father. Some time ago, I saw the error of mine ways and said to mine self, 'If I could find Robin and make amends—'"

"Thou—thou were not doing anything bad to mine because I—I am leaving before then," Robin stuttered.

"I asked thee to marry me, and I apologize for that. Thou wast too young, and at that time, I was not worthy of a good woman. But now I feel that I am. Therefore, I am again asking thee to be mine wife. I make excellent wages and will be able to provide well for thee, Robin."

His words touched her, impressed her. What right had she to hold his youthful rashness against him? And she did want someone to love her, someone to call her own. Her mother, her Quaker guardian, would be glad for such a union. She closed her eyes and envisioned a small cottage of her own, a fireplace, and laughing children.

Marie, cloistered in the other room, kept an ear to the door. She had hoped that Perregrine's heart might arouse to Robin's virtues, but he had sent word by Theodore that she must not let such a hope dwell in her mind. She smothered a sharp disappointment.

"I am only saying no, Theodore," she heard Robin say. "I cannot be marrying anyone until I am finding out first who I am and where I am coming from to this country. It is mine tormenting thought, and I am never being happy until I am knowing. Mine childrens must be knowing the background of their mother."

"When thou lived with us, Robin, I didn't bother to ask, but I am sure I can find out for thee. That is, if Mr.

Schuylhill is yet alive. He probably lives in Jamestown yet. He is the man who brought thee to us."

"From the wrecking of the ship?"

"I'm sorry, mine Robin, I know no details. But if it stands between me and thy marrying to me, I shall find out." Theodore was willing, in the event of Mr. Schuylhill's death, to make up a plausible story. Robin would not know the difference. "I shall be back to call for thee in a few days."

When he left, both Robin and Marie sat in strained silence.

"Do you love him, Robin?" Marie asked at length.

"I am not knowing, Mrs. Abelard. How can one be knowing? Thy son is thinking he is loving Marianne. When he is sickening, he is starting to say he cannot be living without her. But she is not the right one for him. I am knowing it; thou art knowing it. Only he is not knowing it.

"It is the same for mine. I am not knowing that Theodore is the right one for mine. Thou art not knowing if he is the right one for mine, mem. Only Theodore is knowing."

"We must pray, Robin," warned Marie. "God knew what was best for my Perregrine, and He knows what is best for you."

"When I am a child, Theodore is drinking and speaking bad words. He is the meanest of a man. But he is saying that he is changing. How can I be knowing? Words? Words are cheap. Words can be deceiving. I am wanting to see actings."

"You are a wise girl," conceded Marie. "Do not rush into anything."

Before Theodore's return, another trader—one Marie and Robin had never met—brought a letter from Perregrine. He said he hoped that Marie had gotten his first letter, the one he sent by Trader Smyth, and he hoped that Robin had accepted his thanks and had time to consider his proposal. He hoped she was coming.

"What is he meaning, mem?" asked Robin. "Theodore is not bringing us a letter from thy son."

"Nothing makes sense," admitted Marie. "We will ask Mr. Smyth when he returns."

Chapter Twenty-Six

Information

The next time Theodore Smyth came, he wore a diamond stickpin in his lapel. His boots were shinier, his hair plastered with grease even more. Robin was worth the sprucing up, and his appearance had impressed her on his former visit. He didn't intend to lose the petite and pretty raven-haired girl again. She was much more vivacious and more appealing than his first wife.

"Come in and sit a spell, Mr. Smyth," invited Marie, "and have a cup of tea with me." Marie had decided to begin her own detective work on the integrity of Theodore Smyth. Robin must not be chained to a man who would abuse her.

"I've come to get Robin," he said, as if the rules of the game were his and his courtesy would extend only so far.

"Not so fast, Mr. Smyth," Marie chuckled. "She hardly knows you."

Theodore's jaw muscles bunched. "We know each other quite well, Mrs. Abelard. Thou must remember that we shared parents for several years."

"But one changes over the years."

"I have changed. For the better. I will speak to Robin if thou pleasest."

"Robin is at work."

"Where is she working?"

"For one of Lewis's customers. I'm sorry, but I haven't the address."

"The parson is waiting. Robin must go with me today."

"She may not return today."

"What dost thou mean, she may not return today?" With a concerted effort, Theodore held his temper.

"It is a birthing, a new mother. Lewis recommended Robin for the job. Robin is good, and so is the pay."

"I cannot wait." His mouth compressed into a line of irritation. "Thou knowest where she is, and thou wilt not tell me! Thou art hiding her!" His voice rose.

"You are welcome to search the house, Mr. Smyth. I speak the truth."

He jumped up, then sat down again quickly. "Well, thou canst tell her that I found Mr. Schuylhill and got the information about her past. She can worry no more."

"She will want to know, of course."

"She is Mr. Schuylhill's granddaughter. His daughter ran away with a soldier and never returned. On Robin's paternal side, she has Spanish roots."

"There was no shipwreck?"

"No. It is a figment of her imagination, something dramatic that she has dreamed up and wishes to believe. With such a bleak background, she will be most fortunate to get someone like me for a husband."

The discernment with which Marie was gifted told her that Theodore Smyth had created a fabric of falsehood, that he had not been to call on Mr. Schuylhill at all.

"You found the old fellow well?" she asked pleasantly.

"What?" The pause was slight, but Marie caught it. "Oh, yes, yes. He was well. He said to tell his granddaughter hello."

"How is it that all these years he hid from Robin the fact that she was his grandchild?"

"The circumstances of her birth were embarrassing; he thought it best this way." Theodore's tongue was glib and becoming more glib with talking. "He knew that mine mother would train her in a godly manner after the Quaker persuasion. Mine mother would only agree to take Robin under the conditions of secrecy on the grandfather's part."

"That seems strange. Grandparents usually love their grandchildren regardless of their beginnings. Robin couldn't help it that she had an ignoble birth."

Theodore yielded to a cataract of mirth, but there was no gaiety in his laughter. "Stranger things have happened, Mrs. Abelard. Mr. Schuylhill was a proud old codger. He feared that the bad blood would show up in the child."

"I shall insist that Robin visit her grandfather. He may have changed his views."

"Oh, by no means, Mrs. Abelard! It would behoove thee to stay out of this. This is between Robin and mine self. The man is elderly and has a bad heart. To bring an unpleasant recollection into his life now might throw him into apoplexy!" Theodore regretted the tale he had invented, but it was too late to reconstruct it. "When Robin and I are married, I shall see that life is so grand for her she will forget all past skeletons."

"By the way, Mr. Smyth, I have had a most recent message from my son, Perregrine. He says that he sent a letter by you—"

"A letter? I do not recall a letter. It must have been in

the trunk that I took to Lewis's wife. Please check with her. Did your son mention the, uh, the contents of that letter?"

"Only briefly. Of course, he presumed that you had delivered it."

There was a noticeable contrast between Theodore's apologetic reply and the expression on his face. "I am sorry, Mrs. Abelard. The letter of which he speaks must have gotten misplaced."

"Yes, I expect it did." The contempt in Marie's voice was lost on Theodore.

"I will bid thee good day," he said quickly. "I shall check with thee two days hence to see if mine future bride has returned. There will be no more such work for her when we are wed! I shall be the breadwinner."

The bud of a notion blossomed into a fully grown plan in Marie's mind before the day ended. She would launch her own investigation into Robin's past.

The next morning, she asked Lewis to take her to Jamestown to look up a Mr. Schuylhill. "Why, Mother," he teased, "are you calling on a gentleman at your age?"

"I am. And I have my reasons, Lewis," she said.

"I don't know Mr. Schuylhill personally, but Schuyl-hill is a most respected name among the colonies. He has been a philanthropist, I understand. A generous man with a strong sense of duty and a deep love for America. You have made a good choice."

"Lewis! I have no such motives as your imagination conjures up!" she blushed. "This is a *business* call."

Lewis took her to the old-fashioned brownstone house with an "S" on the gate. At first glance, the house was disappointing. It had a big wooden porch with wide and high windows built to allow plenty of light to enter the sitting rooms. Its inconspicuous color blended with the bare earth around it, but the glass panes reflected the day's brilliance with prisms of colors. A perfume of spices hung in the air. They walked up wooden steps, crossed the porch, and entered a chilly parlor.

The butler that answered the clapper said that Mr. Schuylhill's health was poor. According to the doctor, his days were numbered.

"Oh, please, sir," implored Marie. "I must speak with him. It is of utmost importance to—to someone in his family."

The butler hesitated. "I know of no family, ma'am."

"Please, sir."

He shrugged. "It can do no harm. Company might do him good. He has always loved people."

Marie asked Lewis to wait in the drawing room while the butler took her to the bedside of a shrunken man. His withered frame indicated that he may once have been a large person, but now his face was dried and leathery, his eyes a bleached blue. The only flourishing thing about him was his full white beard. It was a strange combination: the majestic flow of hair sprouting from the shriveled face.

"Mr. Schuylhill," Marie began, taking his bony hand. In her strong hands, his were lost and warmed. "I have come to ask a few questions about your grand-daughter."

Mr. Schuylhill held himself stiffly with the exaggerated posture of an old man showing he is not old. It had always saddened Marie to see a man defeated by time. He spoke in a whisper. "I have no granddaughter. I am a bachelor."

"The young lady of whom I speak is Robin."

"Robin?" His dimming eyes lighted, and when he smiled, it was as if a sunset had blazed behind his craggy face, making it suddenly magnificent. "Robin Smyth?"

"Yes. You remember her?"

He was silent for a moment, and then he said, "How could I forget? I *named* her."

"Will you give me her history? It is very important to her just now."

"I supposed that the Smyths would tell her. She has a right to know—"

It took a while for the aged gentleman to get the story told, but Marie listened to every detail. The truth that now unfolded would be ammunition against Theodore Smyth's dishonesty, a release from Robin's prison of apprehension, and a relief to Marie's own mind.

When Mr. Schuylhill finished, Marie thanked him, giving his hand an extra pat. She went home with her mission accomplished. At the appropriate time, she would share the story with Robin.

"Did you make any headway with the old fellow?" Lewis ribbed.

"I did," Marie said. "I am obliged to you for your escort here today, Lewis."

"Any time, Mother. I hope you haven't waited too late. But I have learned that love sometimes revives the most hopeless of humanity." He saw her into her apartment and chuckled his way to his own place. She was a spunky one, his mother. One never knew what she was up to.

Two days later, Theodore Smyth returned. Marie caught a whiff of whiskey on his breath. She was glad that Robin was still gone.

Chapter Twenty-Seven

A Prophecy

"I am wishing I could be talking to Essence," Robin told Marie. "She is a wise woman, a good judge of human character. She is knowing Theodore Smyth from the tradings. He is doing business with her tribe for a much long time."

Marie wore her thoughts on the outside. "Why don't you and I make a trip to the Ayutooks before bad weather sets in, Robin? I would like to see my son, Perregrine, ere the winter gets here. I want to see how his hurt is healing."

"Is thy son not with the Kotopaxis?"

"He is, but Essence will take me to see him, or he can come to see us."

"Lewis will be allowing it?"

"Lewis will fuss, but he will not forbid us to go. He knows how my spirit yearns for my younger son. I will not be leaving him alone; he has Marianne now."

When Marie presented her wishes to Lewis, he arranged for a guide—one who claimed he could make fry bread as tender as a baby's conscience and porridge as hot as the devil's home—to accompany Marie and Robin to their destination. "And please take a message to Essence, Mother," he said. "I have talked with Mr. English about her tribal lands. He is grateful for what she did for his niece, and he sends word that Essence is not to worry. The lands of her tribes will not be disturbed."

Lewis sent them on their way with plenty of supplies for the trip along with gifts for his brother and Essence.

"Bless Marianne," Marie commented to Robin. "She never resents Lewis's generosity. She is making a good daughter-in-law."

"Yes. She is perfect with thy son, Lewis. God is putting them together."

"But my poor Perregrine will never marry."

"Thou mayest be right, mem. Only God is knowing."

Their guide for the trip west was a pleasant fellow who played a fiddle by the campfire at night. The music brought a measure of peace to Robin's troubled soul. The farther they got from the city, the better she felt. The trail seemed to stretch ahead like a beacon to the future. She would get her answer on this trip; when she returned, she would know whether or not she should marry Theodore Smyth. She was anxious to talk to Essence and chafed at the excess of time the guide took for grazing the horses and for cooking.

When they arrived, Marie was surprised that Essence was not surprised to see them. It was almost as if she were expecting them.

"You have come!" she said, throwing her arms about Robin first, then Marie. "Our missionary is waiting with much anticipation."

"How did Perregrine know we were coming?" asked Marie.

"He said that when you got his letter with the invitation and the explanation, you would come."

"We—we didn't get such a letter."

"Then why did you come to us?"

"We came because we wanted to see you and Perregrine."

Essence smiled broadly. "That is even better!"

Marie took to her elk-skin cot early, but Robin was anxious to talk with Essence, to confide in her, to find answers.

"I am coming to be asking thee questions," she said. "I have been missing thee so much!"

"What bothers you, my little Robin?"

"The marrying."

"Oh, my dear child! There is nothing to fret about! You will be a most happy wife. I saw it when you were here caring for our Reverend Abelard."

"Thou know well the man whom is asking mine, Essence?"

"There's no better man anywhere, Robin. He is a true man of God."

"He is saying that he is changing."

"Yes. He has changed."

"Thou hast done much trading with him?"

"Trading?"

"Often he is coming to trade?"

Essence puckered her brow. "I don't understand what you mean by trading."

"The furs and the skins."

"No, he doesn't—"

"Once he is coming here while I am here with thee. Then he is not knowing whom I am. Only he is learning, and now he is asking twice that I am marrying him."

"Twice?"

"I am telling him that I cannot be wedding until I am

finding who mine self is. He is promising to find out soon what is mine nationality from the sea. He is returning with the knowing for me when I am going back to Philadelphia."

Essence was thoroughly confused.

"But, my Essence, I am not knowing if I am loving him—or if he is loving mine in truth. How am I to be knowing?"

"I am not following you, Robin. You are right that Mr. Abelard did not know who held his hand when he was sick, but—"

"Thou art happy for mine to be marrying Theodore Smyth then?"

"Theodore Smyth?"

"He is asking for mine hand."

"No! No! Robin! He drinks the white man's fire-water! His temper is a demon. Why would you think to marry such a wicked man?"

"He is saying he is all changing now."

"He means well, Robin. Yet it takes but a puff of temptation, and he is mad with alcohol."

"He is my family, but nothing akin. He is asking mine to wife when I am much young. I am running away from him. But he is finding me these two months ago, and he will not be hearing me saying no. I *will* be marrying him, he is saying."

"Robin, the man already has a wife! And a child. This was told to me by another trader who knows him well. He mistreated his good wife, then left her. Why would you want such an evil man for a husband?"

Tears budded behind Robin's eyes. "I am not knowing any of this, mine Essence. This is why I am coming all the way here for thine advising. God is speaking with thy tongue to mine self. Oh, Essence, I need thy help! I need thy praying! I need thy loving! Please do not unlove me for mine ignorance!"

Essence folded the girl into her arms. "Oh, Robin! Robin! I love you more than ever. You are like my own daughter. God sent you to me so that I could guide you aright. You shall *not* marry Theodore Smyth! God has a beautiful plan for you, and it is about to unfold. I marvel at His ways!"

"Thank thee for thy caring, mine Essence. Maybe I cannot be going back to the city. I am not wanting to see Theodore ever any more."

"Tomorrow we will send for the missionary, and we shall see what God will do for all of us."

Essence did not realize the import of her own prophecy.

Chapter Twenty-Eight

Confession

The missionary greeted his mother, but Perregrine's eyes caught Robin's as compellingly as if he had seized her hands. Standing quietly in a posture of natural grace, wearing a simple, gray wool dress, long black hair pinned back—setting off the olive smoothness of her skin—was the most beautiful, the most desirable girl he had ever seen. Here was the girl who sat beside him faithfully throughout his death-threatening illness. And her beauty was more than physical; the beauty of holiness rested upon her.

Something strangely new, inexpressibly sweet, coursed through Perregrine's veins when Robin looked into his eyes. Nothing he felt for Marianne compared with this. This was *right*.

"Hello, Robin," he said.

Robin felt the emotional impact too, but she held herself in strict reserve. Perregrine had loved Marianne, and in his delirium he had said that he could not live without her. Those words still haunted Robin. She could

191

not lose her heart to a man who would not be able to return her devotion. When one didn't know one's own background, one was frightened at what reaction, braided into the ancestry, might leak out unexpectedly. "Hello, Mr. Abelard, sir," she said. "I am glad to see thee well."

Perregrine's attempts at courtship were awkward. He had no idea how to woo Robin, yet he knew he must win her. It had been easier with Marianne. He had only to satisfy Marianne's craving for *things*. Robin was different. A nosegay of wildflowers meant as much to her as a jeweled brooch. It didn't take material comforts to make her happy. She had spent a lifetime empty of possessions; the fountain of her happiness sprang from a deeper source.

He soon learned that Robin liked for him to talk about his missionary work. She sat at rapt attention, drinking in every detail. She was absorbed with his vision. With her glowing eyes riveted to him and her lips parted, Perregrine knew she was the loveliest creature he had ever seen. However, he convinced himself that if he moved too fast she would bolt.

"I would like to be going with Essence to this tribe of thy missionarying. I would like to be meeting Lithia and her son and the chief," she said one day.

"Then I will tell Essence to bring you over," Perregrine said with a poor stab at casualness. "And I will show you the pueblo that the tribe is building for me. I am now their pastor."

"Oh, it is wonderful!" She clapped her hands in girlish anticipation, and Perregrine was sure he would turn handsprings to gain her delight again and again.

"They are my people, and I will return to them soon," he said. "I would like for you and my mother and Essence to go with me."

"I would love to do that," Robin said with artless simplicity. "But is a long way?"

"It is not far. Only a two-day journey. One night we will be without a dwelling."

"I am enjoying the skies and the outside of travel."

The forest they traveled through to reach the Kotopaxi tribe was thick with trees jostling for growing room, darkening the path with their umbrellas of leaves. Fiddle-head ferns ran rampant. The air was pleasantly fresh and cool when they made camp for the night, but Essence kept sniffing. "Rain," she said.

Sometime during the night, Robin awoke to the crashing of thunder. A flashing spear of light split the sky, illuminating the blackness. Rain fell, lading the foliage with water until the trees could hold no more and dumped their contents on the campers below. Above them, leaves that twirled and fell on them were torn from their branches, the sounds of their snapping dimmed by the wail of the wind and hammer of the rain.

This was nature's might, and it thrilled Robin. She was not afraid. Then at a time between night and dawn when shapes have no detail, someone crept up and spread a coat over Robin. Toward dawn the rain stopped and the wind lost its violence—and Robin saw that the coat was Perregrine's.

Robin immediately lassoed the hearts of the Kotopaxi tribesmen. They called her "the sweet flower." Victor, Lithia's teenage son, was especially pleased to have guests. His attentiveness rather bewildered Robin. Being honored was a new experience for her; she had always served.

Victor was a perceptive boy, and it didn't take him long to perceive the missionary's distraction. Something was disturbing his hero, eating at his vitals. His face was troubled. Whatever the problem, Victor determined to fix it.

The boy silently followed Perregrine into the dappled shadows of the beech woods the following morning. They had learned to communicate well, the white man and the Indian boy, despite the language barrier. "Why are you sad?" Victor traced a trail down his cheek with his finger to indicate tears.

The splendor of the morning with the sun filtering through the branches mocked Perregrine's mood. "It is the Sweet Flower," admitted Perregrine, reaching down to pick a wild moon flower as an illustration. He was glad to have someone to listen to his confession. "My heart is longing for her, but I do not know if her heart is longing for me."

"Wait here," motioned Victor. "I will bring her to you." Perregrine understood that he was to wait, but the remainder of Victor's plan was unclear. Had he known his young friend's intent, he would have left on winged feet.

Soon Victor returned with a distressed Robin. "Thou art injuring thyself, sir?" she asked.

Perregrine was taken aback. Her soft voice, her solicitation flustered him the more. "No, Miss Robin, I—I came here to meditate and pray, and Victor followed me."

"He is concerned for thee. Can I be helping?"

Perregrine didn't speak but simply stood looking at her in what seemed a paralysis of despair. Every movement she made seemed to him precious, unique, and adorably feminine.

In that look, Robin saw the lonely man that Perregrine was. She found herself pulled apart by compassion . . . and something else. What was it? Not jealousy, no. It was resentment. She found herself resenting Marianne, the selfish girl who cared more for her own comforts than she cared for the man who risked his life to save her. He had loved her, but he had thrown his pearls before swine, and his love had been trampled underfoot.

"I am not free to speak of the burden on my heart," Perregrine said at last.

"I would be pleased to listen, Mr. Abelard."

"Please call me Perregrine, Robin."

"Yes, Perregrine, sir."

Now was as good a time as any. Perregrine could bear the suspense no longer. If Robin rejected him, it would hurt, but it would be over. He must know if there was any chance for him.

"I—I didn't know that it was you who sat beside me and—and held my hand when I was ill."

Robin didn't flinch. "I was glad to."

"Now I know that God sent you into my life for a purpose. His loving, wise Spirit arranged that we find each other. Your coming to me was in His mind, in His plan. I want you to marry me, Robin." There, he had said it.

When she didn't move, Perregrine came to stand before her. He took her hand in his. "You, Robin, are the wife God has sent for me. You are the woman to walk beside me in my missionary work." He cupped her chin in his hand very carefully, with no haste, nothing to cause her fright. As he looked into her eyes, she looked back steadily—her look brought panic to his soul. She would refuse him!

"I cannot be forgetting what thou art saying when thy head is gone to the fever," she said, turning her face away so that he could not see the tears that swam there.

"Oh, Robin," he groaned pitifully. "What did I say?"

"Thou art saying, 'Marianne, Marianne, I cannot be living without—' and then thou art not finishing. I am not for taking her place, please, sir."

"Dearest Robin!" He smiled at her even though his

195

cheeks were wet. "I remember trying to get that sentence out. I had been near to death and close to eternity. I felt that God had given me the gift of life and I owed my service to Him. I was trying to tell Marianne that I could not live without *fulfilling my call as a missionary.*

"Essence tried to show me the error of my ways and that I would never be happy if I gave up my work for God. But I had pledged myself to become Marianne's husband, and I would not go back on my honor. I realize now that I did not love her, but so greatly did I want someone to love—and someone who would love me as much—that I was disappointed when she left me for my brother.

"It is you that I love, Robin."

Chapter Twenty-Nine

Glorious Finale

A blazing flash of joy shot through Robin. Perregrine, the great missionary and man of God, had said that he loved her. Yet some niggling torment suddenly dampened her pure joy.

"I must be thinking. I must be praying," she told Perregrine, pulling her hand away. "Thou must be praying alike."

"You cannot love me?"

The question almost broke Robin's heart. "I can be loving thee, oh, so much, Perregrine. Much more than I can ever be telling. I can be proud to be the wife of a missionary. But I am not feeling worthy. I am feeling no good enough."

"You are an angel, Robin!"

"Thou art in store of a beautiful future and maybe childrens. I am not even knowing my past for them. I am asking God one time that if He is wanting mine to be marrying that He is finding mine past for me. I am telling Him that I will never be marrying until I am finding who I am from the ocean. I cannot be breaking my vow."

"I see."

"Maybe when I am coming again, I will be knowing. . . ."

Perregrine's declaration of love went with Robin back to the Indian camp. It lay down with her at night and arose with her in the morning. She couldn't escape it. If only . . .

Marie noticed that Perregrine looked haggard and wretched. And Robin's eyes were dull; she walked about stricken and wordless. Marie half suspected the problem. They were in love, but there was an unseen barrier. What could she do to help the two people she loved more than she loved her own life?

Essence, Marie, and Robin made preparations to return to the Ayutooks. From there Robin and Marie would travel back to Philadelphia. Perregrine felt that his heart would shatter. He had promised to do God's will and had been at such peace about Robin, so assured that God had let him know what to do. His decision to marry Robin had seemed utterly right, so beautiful, so blessed. And now she was leaving.

The night before their departure, they met in Lithia's pueblo for a time of fellowship. For Essence, the visit held a bittersweet ending. She knew of Perregrine's affection for the orphaned girl, and she discerned Robin's yearning for love too. They were each stranded on their separate and lonely islands. Essence had no family; Robin had no family. Perregrine needed a wife. And there was Theodore Smyth to fear. Essence was a forthright person, and she knew it would be hard for her to keep her silence about these problems.

She couldn't. And she didn't. "I was hoping that you would ask Robin to stay with us," Essence addressed her remark to Perregrine, and her meaning was clear.

"I did," he said.

"And you will not stay, Robin?" pressed Essence gently.

"I am wanting so much to stay," Robin said, baring her feelings honestly. "But I am promising God that I will not be marrying any man until I am finding mine past. It is no fair to a husband that I am searching forever for mine self. I cannot then be a good wife with a whole heart."

Marie jerked to attention. "But, Robin! I know all about your past!" she exclaimed.

"Mem, thou art never telling me."

"I had planned to, and then we got caught up in planning our trip. I am truly sorry, Robin—"

"It is so bad that thou cannot be sharing it with our friends?"

"It isn't bad at all, Robin. It is magnificent!"

"Where are you finding my beginnings?"

"Your foster brother, Theodore Smyth, returned while you were working for one of Lewis's customers. He had been drinking. He said that he had visited a Mr. Schuylhill and learned of your past. The story Theodore told was twisted and sordid. Something told me it wasn't true, that Theodore had not talked to Mr. Schuylhill at all. His fabrication was invented to make you feel cheap and on the level of a wine bibber.

"So I made a trip to visit Mr. Schuylhill myself."

Excitement gripped Robin. "Thou art doing this for mine? Oh, Mrs. Abelard, thou art precious!"

"And I did it for *me*," smiled Marie. "Mr. Schuylhill was a very aged fellow with a bushy white beard."

"He is the man who is pulling me from the waters!"

"He is. But not from the ocean. He found you on a creek bank, clinging to a log. Beside you was a small boy who may have been your brother. He had been drowned. Mr. Schuylhill considers it a miracle that you had clung to the log for so long. He named you Robin because you reminded him of a wet bird. He was a bachelor, so he took you to his neighbor, a Quaker lady by the name of Smyth. She fell in love with you at once.

"They didn't know how far you had floated, but there was a flood that washed away an entire Indian tribe further west. Mr. Schuylhill said he always figured that you were one of the few survivors of that tribe. He couldn't recall the tribe's name."

Essence reached for her throat. Her voice came out in a thin quiver. "Did—did the man say what *year* he found Robin?"

"That was seventeen years ago. He guessed her to be three or four years old at that time. She spoke no English."

A cry, half joy, half disbelief, escaped the lips of the Indian woman. "Seventeen years ago, many of our tribe were lost, washed away in a flood. My two children, a boy and a girl, ages three and four, were swept away—"

The dawning came, suddenly and illuminating, for both mother and daughter.

"My Amora, my precious one!" shrieked Essence. "It is you!"

"Mema!" shouted Robin. "My own real mema!"

Essence flung her arms about Robin. She began to croon the song she had sung to her child in early cradleboard days. "My precious one is sleeping. I will rock my precious one. . . ." From the far reaches of her memory, Robin found the words to join her mother as they sang together in their native tongue. Their tears mingled in a happy mother-and-daughter reunion. Perregrine thought it was the loveliest harmony he had ever heard.

"Why didn't we see it?" scolded Lithia. "We are blind! They *look* alike! The *eyes*!" Essence interpreted her message to Marie, Robin, and Perregrine.

"Yes," Marie said. "The eyes. They are the same."

Perregrine's face split with a glorious smile. "Now, my Robin, my sweet Amora, does this mean that you will be my wife?"

"I will be the best wife in the world. I am so happy forever. God is answering mine prayers so prettily. At last, I am finding mine family! And mine rootings are in honor! I am never being so much happy before. I am having the most loving husband, the sweetest mother, the—?" she nodded toward Lithia.

"Aunt Lithia."

"And don't forget about Cousin Victor," the boy reminded.

"Or Uncle Chieftain," the chief grinned.

Robin walked over to Perregrine and kissed the bridge of his nose. "But first—and as quickly as possible—is *Mrs. Missionary Abelard*! It is the steppings of my Lord's order."

About the Author

LAJOYCE MARTIN, a minister's wife, has written for Word Aflame Publications for many years with numerous stories and books in print. She is in much demand for speaking at seminars, banquets, and camps. Her writings have touched people young and old alike all over the world.

Other Books by LaJoyce Martin:

The Harris Family Saga:
To Love a Bent-Winged Angel
Love's Mended Wings
Love's Golden Wings
When Love Filled the Gap
To Love a Runaway
A Single Worry
Two Scars Against One
The Fiddler's Song

Pioneer Romance Series:
So Swift the Storm
So Long the Night

Pioneer Romance:
The Wooden Heart
Heart-Shaped Pieces
Light in the Evening Time

Western:
The Other Side of Jordan
To Even the Score

Path of Promise:
The Broken Bow
Ordered Steps

Children's Short Stories:
Batteries for My Flashlight

Nonfiction:
Mother Eve's Garden Club
Heroes, Sheroes, and a Few Zeroes

Order from:
Pentecostal Publishing House
8855 Dunn Road
Hazelwood, MO 63042-2299